M.K. DEPPNER

A Rare Find

Magpie Press

For Matthew, Bella, and Olivia

Chapter 1

He'd taken to calling it The Attic Project. Not creative in the slightest, but Samuel Reid knew where his talents lay. And they lay neither in creative names nor cleaning out attics. They lay in selling seven- and eight-figure real estate typically not found on this continent and a hands-on project or two when the occasion called for it. And there was one thing of which Samuel Reid was certain: he knew what he wanted. Women, real estate, clothes, money. It was that simple.

Until it wasn't. Until he woke up in Paris the morning after a sale so large, he should have felt nothing but elation. Instead, he felt nothing, and he'd wanted nothing to do with the celebratory festivities or the woman he'd woken up next to.

So, he'd given it all up.

And what had he gotten in return?

He knew what he'd gotten. Though it was night when he'd

1

arrived, he'd felt it on the descent into the area. Somehow, the scent of the Flint Hills, that prairie musk, had filled the cockpit before he'd even touched down. It brought memories rushing back. Memories of college and visiting his grandparents and that feeling that he was a teenager again, and life was full of possibility. And when he'd stepped down from the plane and into the damp night air, he'd felt it. The crickets and cicadas sang it.

The place he had come to was now his home.

Trying to shake that feeling of permanence, he thought of his plane parked on the short tarmac at the regional airport, gathering dust and tumbleweeds. There was nothing permanent about this if he didn't want it to be, and he could fly anywhere at a moment's notice should the opportunity arise. He could rent a hangar if this became a long-term stay.

He hadn't been back in town long, and honestly, he had no idea what he was doing there. Retiring at forty-two, what was he thinking? He had tried forcing himself to work after he'd sold that ritzy flat to Juliette and Felicia in Paris. And despite the millions in savings and investments and properties spread across four continents, it brought him no joy.

It had become something it hadn't been when he started. That was the long and short of it. Sure, the money was attractive, but the real worth was in the beautiful architecture and locales. Money could buy anything, and he felt like he'd seen it all. Rooftop terraces become organic jungles, mirrors and glass surfaces with integrated screens, heated living room floors, views of the Eiffel Tower, all of it. And then he'd become numb to it all.

Real estate had completely lost its charm. Just like that. Overnight.

So, he'd sold his properties over a two-week period and made his way back to Warren, Kansas. There, in a place where no one remembered him, he felt untethered and adrift but no longer like he wanted to throw himself out of an airplane over the Atlantic. He felt like he'd come home for the first time in almost two decades.

And of course, his grandfather didn't let him sit still for long. Patrick had the energy of a man a third his age and a wit ten times as sharp. Samuel had a hard time keeping up with him.

So, when his grandfather mentioned a business venture in the attic, Samuel was concerned that he was looking to divvy up his property in light of his advancing age. Nana had rolled her eyes at them and settled into her overstuffed blue chair with the day's crossword. Apparently, all was normal in the Reid household.

His grandfather had a bit of everything stuffed into the attic, but books were far and away the majority of what was up there. And they were in fine condition—they had escaped the dust and spiders plaguing most of the stifling room. Patrick had tended to these books with special care, whether he admitted it or not.

Nana had mentioned going to estate sales with his grandfather, but Samuel hadn't known just how lucrative this sidehustle was until now. And now it was time to get these books onto the market again. Patrick had said Samuel's retirement was as good a cause as any.

Samuel sifted through a box. He knew nothing about old and rare books. He could tell they were in perfect condition, but that was it. He was uneasy that they had been stored in the attic—wasn't that bad for books?

"Grandpa?"

The man ignored him. Samuel sighed, "Patrick?"

"Yes, my boy?"

Samuel shook his head. He had to try every once in a while, just to see, but he was hardly surprised that it was still all business, as it had been since he was a teenager. "You found all of these at estate sales?"

One volume from 1816 had a garage sale price sticker for two dollars on it. Samuel peeled it off carefully and was thankful no sticky residue remained. Somehow, he didn't think anyone interested in buying the book would appreciate that.

Patrick, bent over another box, looked up. His hazel eyes were a mirror of his grandson's as they flicked between the book and Samuel's face. "You recall that I asked you to come here for a business opportunity, yes?"

"Yes." His grandfather had actually laughed when Samuel told him he'd retired—a full-on belly laugh he'd never heard come out of the man before. It had left him bewildered and feeling quite salty toward his grandfather.

"You're going to sell those books for me."

Samuel must've had an incredulous look on his face because Patrick threw a sour look right back. "Don't you look at me like that, young man. I've been at this a while longer than you and I know there's a bit of money to be had in this."

"Fine, I'll play. How much and what all do you need me to do?"

"Books, lad, are worth a fortune if you have the right ones. There are collectors and museums all over the world looking for some of these books. Museums, collectors, fight over certain publications, certain runs, books from certain eras."

"Sounds like a niche market." Samuel grabbed one of three books which were together inside a box. *The Woman in White.*

4

He'd never heard of it.

Patrick pointed to the gilded cardboard the set had been encased in. "With the box, that set is worth at least three grand. Our cut."

Samuel just about dropped it back into the box. "Three grand," he parroted stupidly. He remembered the crappy mass-market paperbacks he'd read voraciously as a kid. The two ideas didn't compute.

Patrick shrugged. "That set is. There are more collections here worth triple. And there are enough collectors out there to make it worth it. Your job is to farm out these books to various bookstores in the area that cater to rare books and their upsell. I don't want one of them to have all of them. Creates more interest, more rivalry."

"Can't you do that yourself?"

"I'm old, boy, and these have sat in my attic long enough. I'll give you twenty percent."

He couldn't believe he was doing this. He'd come here for some peace and quiet. What should he expect from the man who'd given him a silk tie for his fourteenth birthday and told him it was time to start dressing like a real man? "Fifty. And that'll add up to what?"

Patrick worked his mouth and frowned. Samuel felt like an intimidated boy again.

"Twenty-five. And I'll make sure you get a handful of zeros."

"You're joking, old man. Forty."

Patrick gritted his teeth and sneered. "How about I make sure it's six figures? Give it some time, though. Take it or leave it."

"Seriously? I'm happy to help you out short term for some pocket change, but I won't hold my breath for that kind of money."

Patrick's sneer deepened. "Didn't they teach you how to schmooze a deal in business school, boy?"

"When the deal was fair and honest, they did." Samuel sighed. "Listen, I'll help you out for a few weeks, okay? Then I'm off to other things. I've just got to get myself sorted here. I'll help, though."

They shook on it. So much for relaxing and melting into a puddle on the couch.

Chapter 2

The bookstore hadn't been this busy in the eight years Melanie Montgomery had been there. And it was unusual. She expected rushes in early spring and when the school year ended, but late summer a few weeks before first semester started? The crowd at yesterday's author signing should have been a red flag. She'd hoped for down time that evening to watch *Jauja* or maybe *The Conformist*. But even the lure of getting lost in a movie was overshadowed by how much work she had to do tonight.

Whatever was in the air, everyone in town had decided that this was the day to clean out their attics, garages, and basements, and bring in their old books. If she saw another *Fifty Shades of Grey* book, she was going to scream. She had lost count of how many people she had turned away because Poor Oliver's had too many copies. She suggested bringing them back in a month or two, but she rarely saw those faces again. The books probably ended up at Goodwill.

The story repeated itself. A month after a blockbuster was

released, the used copies poured in, and then the crowd would get amped up again when another sequel came out. It was an art as much as it was a science to determine how many copies to keep for people seeking seconds—like-new books marked down to used bookstore prices.

It hadn't looked too bad when she'd opened Poor Oliver's doors that morning. The sun had been out, and it was muggy, but late morning had arrived and so did the people. An older gentleman came in with two giant suitcases full of paperbacks, followed by three harassed-looking mothers with boxes of books and children in tow. One child had gone full bore into the diverse authors' table at the front and knocked towers of books onto the floor.

Yet, even for the bustle, she settled into its rhythm, enjoying the people as much as the books. Small talk came to her easily, and she loved peeking into others' lives through their book piles.

She smiled and happily took a stack of cookbooks from a middle-aged woman who reminded her of her mother. She helped a young woman looking for books on photography and Warren's history around the turn of the century—followed later by Professor Monroe who wanted the same history books.

There must be a class on campus. She made a mental note to check her inventory for history or photography books to put out. Maybe she'd even spruce that section for better presentation. Yes, today was a good day.

During the lunchtime lull, she rearranged a shelf by one of the front picture windows. It looked cozy at night with soft lamplight falling upon the displayed books and silk flowers, but the shadows were off in the bright afternoon sun. Happily humming to herself, she tapped her foot against the base of the display as she worked, pausing when the sun disappeared behind massive gray clouds. It was deep summer, and a late afternoon shower or storm wasn't unusual. At least with the university relatively empty, there wouldn't be droves of college students loitering in the tiled foyer to escape the rain.

The clouds held her captivated. Were they more blue or gray or purple? Enclosed as she was in the front display, the sky didn't feel so large and oppressive. Here, she had a slice of it all to herself. She was vaguely aware that Paul had entered and stood at display behind her, but he was quiet in the moment with her—his solid form friendly and comforting.

He whistled softly, some bird call or another to lull her back to reality. She swiveled to look at him.

"Looks like it's going to storm," she said. Paul helped her climb out of her spot.

His smile was easy and never serious. "Mmm, yep. Good thing you get to stay inside all day."

"And you don't? How long can you stay today? I have a long list I need help with." She wiped her hands on her store shirt and headed back to the register to find her list for Paul. "Did you bring me lunch? Please say you did. I can't go upstairs and eat another turkey sandwich. Not this week."

He grinned and set a brown bag next to the register. She peeked inside and her mouth watered at the sight of the pasta salad from Walnut Café. "Hell yes! Thank you!"

Paul laughed on an exhale and began moving heavier boxes of "new" arrivals to the sorting area. "I swear you're more excited about people bringing you food than going to get it yourself. They have a great patio area, you know."

Melanie smiled, but her stomach twisted at his statement.

"You know I like eating here."

Paul smiled, the eye-rolling gone. "I know. And no pressure. Just saying."

"I know," she replied. But it was pressure. She didn't like thinking about sitting on a patio eating food. Food appeared and she ate it. Paul brought it. Anna Jane brought it from the Walnut Cafe. But now she was thinking about where it came from. Outside.

She changed the subject before she bit into food that she no longer wanted. "Can you help me measure this afternoon? I think we're going to have to rearrange for the new shelves, but I want to make sure."

Business had been good enough lately that she could finally spring for some more reclaimed bookshelves, but first, she needed to know if she had space for them. With the regular school year employees not coming back for at least another week, she needed any help from Paul she could get. Then there was the painting that was—if she was being honest—never going to get done, then stripping and refinishing the staircase banisters, and finding a few more rugs to protect the wood floor where the new bookshelves would go. Someday she needed to strip and refinish the floor, too, but she'd have to shut down for at least a week—and work up the nerve to stay somewhere else for a week.

Paul shrugged, unusually coy. "I've got a few hours, then I have to go work on other projects."

"Other projects, Paul? Are their names Bren and Stephanie?" A few customers came in and Melanie called a *hello* to them before turning her attention back to Paul.

"Don't tell me I'm wrong."

"You're not."

"I knew it. I thought you said you and Brenna broke up again?"

Paul kicked the already scuffed corner of the counter. "We didn't break up. We're just taking a break."

Melanie rolled her eyes. "Just be single, it's not that bad. I know you're a young'un, but—"

"Young'un, my ass, I'm only four years younger than you."

Melanie threw him a look. "Four years is ages in the dating world. Can you take the book carts outside for me?"

"And yet we're not that different, for being four years apart," he replied. He rolled a cart laden with fifty-cent paperbacks toward the front doors.

Melanie rolled her eyes. "Please don't start that. Definitely not."

But she thought about it the rest of the afternoon. She'd had a brief fling with Paul back before she set her sights on the bookstore, but it had been no more than that. She cherished their friendship more than the three times she'd kissed him.

Still. She'd been single since then. But that was about the time she found the bookstore. And she felt inexorably entwined with the bookstore's success after the fire and rebuilding. Every decision since then had been hers alone. Melanie glanced around. The tall bookcases looked back at her in their mishmash of golden honeys and darker mahoganies. They would be there, steady and strong for her. All that she wanted and needed was here.

The storm never did come. It felt like a tease, a denial of some release she was searching for. As she locked the front doors, she caught the scent of rain in the air. For a moment, it smelled like pure nature, but then scents of the surrounding buildings—food and asphalt and trash—rushed in to cover it up.

Melanie sighed and flipped the light switch off at the front, then checked the lights in the displays. Satisfied that everything was as it should be, she trekked over to the staircase against the back wall that led to her living area. As she did every night, she unclipped the rope with the sign that stated OWNER'S-PRIVATE, reclipped it behind her, and headed upstairs.

Chapter 3

S he was kneeling in the classics section shelving copies of *Jane Eyre* when the storm blew in the next afternoon. The sun had been gone a while before the rain started, but it grew so dark that it looked more like late evening. It'd likely be a typical summer storm that raged for an hour or two and then left, making way for a humid evening. She could turn on the radio in case there was hail, though there was really nothing she could do for the roof and windows at the store. She was thankful she didn't have a vehicle to worry about.

From her spot on the College Heights Road side of the store, she could watch the heavy rain begin. Poor Oliver's was quiet, the weather bringing a welcome break to the abnormal stream of customers unloading their weekend cleaning. No one had come in for a bit, save for the guy who always lingered longer than he should while asking random, absurd questions.

Moments after the wind really picked up, the front doors blew open on a gust of wind and spray. The first thing she saw were his loafers. Her eyebrows shot up into her bangs. *Did UGG make men's loafers?*

If they did, they came in men's, fuzzy, size 12 and all. They were soaked through and the rain hadn't stopped there. His bootcut jeans were wet halfway up his calves. *Muscular calves*, she clarified, appreciating the way the wet denim stuck to his legs. His feet squished over her clean tile as he headed toward the counter.

He was handsome—yes—and his rain-soaked t-shirt made him look like he'd just stepped out of one of her foreign films. Like a scene in the rain where the man's chasing after his woman, desperate to get her back, screaming something poetic and full of longing in Italian. Dark hair was plastered to his forehead. She wondered if it was brown and wavy when it was dry. His eyes tracked from left to right, looking, she supposed, for…well, *her*, given the bag of books he carried.

Tortoiseshell glasses slipped from his nose. Her eyes wandered up his arms. He wore a navy blue t-shirt that fit just a bit too tight around his tanned arms. He definitely knew his way around a weight room, and anyone with that kind of time was bound to be trouble. What was he doing with a bag of books? Probably bringing them in for someone else. She checked his left hand. No ring. Maybe a girlfriend. But those sopping loafers. Had he meant to leave the house that way? Her Italian Romeo surely wouldn't.

She stood from her hidden position and went to help him. "Can I take those for you?"

He turned toward her, and her amusing thoughts were brought to an abrupt halt. He had a face that deserved to be in an Austen novel. A pair of hazel eyes caught hers and stilled everything around her. Hair that was just too long stuck to his ears and meticulously groomed stubble peppered his jaw and chin. Even for the uber casual look, the watch that adorned his wrist screamed money.

Mr. Darcy visiting the country, she thought, her lips twitching into an involuntary smile. At first glance, the tortoiseshell glasses decidedly did not fit on the moodily handsome face looking back at her. But she liked them. Maybe Mr. Darcy would have worn glasses like this had they existed then. Melanie reined in the errant thoughts. What was she doing? Trying to turn this man into a late-Regency, early Victorian Romeo? Everyone knew how *that* story ended anyway. She couldn't get control of herself today. Must be the weather.

He didn't seem to notice her stare. He pushed wet hair from his forehead and handed over the wet bag of books. "Thank you. I can't believe I got caught in that—no warning or anything."

She accepted the bag, hoping the books inside weren't ruined. Not that Poor Oliver's really had much more space for the inevitable standard reads in this bag. He had to be from out of state—no warning? Really? Anyone with a pair of eyes should have noticed the ominous clouds.

Something flapping outside the door caught her eye and her heart dropped in her chest. "Oh, no!" she exclaimed. "The wind! My book carts!"

She tossed the bag onto the counter and dashed toward the doors. She kicked off her shoes and hastily rolled her jeans up to her knees. It probably didn't matter, but it would be nice if at least one part of her wasn't wet by the time she got back in. For a long, slow moment, she was ten again and going through the same motion before she waded into the creek that ran behind her parents' house. So strong was the memory that when she stepped into the vestibule between the interior and exterior doors, she half expected to feel warm summer mud squishing between her toes instead of rain-splashed tile beneath her heels.

But at the outside doors, she stopped dead. Why had Paul pushed the carts so far *outside*? They looked like they were leagues away, impossible to reach on the sidewalk, and not even under the awning.

The memory of wading through the creek blinked out of existence as something else took its place. It rose within her like a black mud bubble, and she thought suddenly that she wished she could stretch out her arms and summon the book carts to her, to pull them back inside with her mind. She wished it so hard. But she simply stood there, staring at her books getting soaked.

"Can I help you?" The voice startled her so fully that she jumped. She'd forgotten that Mr. Handsome was even there.

"Please!" Even through her panic, she worried how that might sound. Whiny? Desperate? Fear was bubbling up inside her. It was easier *not* to think about going outside, but now that she was forced to, it seemed like her world might implode at any second.

Mr. Handsome jogged into the rain without a word of complaint or acknowledgement that she'd done anything wrong.

A violent burst of wind grabbed the door from Melanie's grasp and hit her with a hard gust of rain. She nearly stumbled over the threshold but caught herself before she stepped outside. The fear and panic were instantaneous, and the carts were groaning in protest.

"You have to unlock the wheels!" Melanie called over the

wind and rain. She mimed reaching down and flipping the locks on the wheels.

He did as she said, moving quickly to push each cart under the awning. She watched in fascination at how fluidly he moved his tall form, despite being hampered by ruined loafers. They squished comically with every step.

"These are heavy. I'm glad I was here to help,"

Melanie felt her face flush. She didn't know what was worse—that he thought she'd needed help because she wasn't capable or that she couldn't say why she really couldn't go outside herself. "Thank you. I mean, I'm sorry you had to do that. You got wet again."

"I'm more worried about the books than my hair." The way his eyes sparkled when he said that, the humor in his voice, slid its way through the mess of her thoughts. That was interesting.

The books were soaked, though. Damn it.

When he was close enough with the first cart, she pulled it toward the interior doors too hard and hit the metal threshold. She watched in horror as the cart tipped and books tumbled onto the entrance's wet tile.

But suddenly Mr. Handsome was there, grabbing the cart before the entire enterprise tipped over. She watched in almost stupid awe as the muscles in his forearms and biceps flexed as he easily righted an obviously heavy object. Before that moment, Melanie would have vehemently disagreed with anyone who might hint that she was a sucker for a strong man. But to watch this muscular man so effortlessly react... his arms straining the sleeves of his t-shirt...well, she felt weak and hopelessly female.

And irritated.

She gritted her teeth and smiled. "Thank you," she said more coolly than she intended. "I can manage from here. This is my job."

He held the door as she pushed through the entry. She brushed by him and smelled something deep and earthy. It was like books and patchouli and rain. She might have drooled if not for how foolish and aggravated she felt.

By the time she had turned around to grab the other cart, he was already pushing it inside. She felt instant relief when all the doors were shut again. The outside was all outside again. She was safe.

"Thank you, but you really don't have to do that." Handsome and irritating. Could he not take simple instructions?

He parked the cart next to the first row of fiction and again pushed the hair from his forehead. It stuck up from his head in such a way that Melanie wanted to reach over and smooth it down. That was irritating too.

He smiled, and his face went from dark and brooding to friendly in an instant. "It's nothing. I hate to see those books get wet."

She stared at the carts. They were only fifty cent paperbacks, and Poor Oliver's had multiple copies of each. They would dry, she would have a damage sale. People would still buy them. But still. She was upset that she'd gotten distracted and hadn't thought about what she should be doing for her business.

Chapter 4

Melanie stalked back to the sales counter and grabbed a roll of paper towels. She ripped a few sheets off for herself, then offered them to him. He took them, watching her with quiet interest.

"Where are you from?" she asked, trying to shift his attention away from herself.

He tousled his hair and shimmering raindrops scattered. The result was as drool-worthy as the rest of him. "Near here, originally. Nemaha. I'm in town from Vancouver, though."

"Traveling professor?" Melanie ventured as she finished drying at least some of her face and arms. Her hair was soaked, but she wasn't going to towel off in front of this guy. She felt keyed up after running into the rain and watching his unintended show of strength. Whatever edge the storm had taken away was chiseled sharp again by the openly curious gaze this man had for her.

"Actually, just visiting my grandparents."

Well, that was adorable. "Oh. Can I look at the books you've brought?" she asked, trying to find some sense of normalcy.

She pulled the bag closer and set to doing the work she loved. What would this bag of books tell her about the gentleman before her?

People discarded books for a million reasons—space, boredom, desire for more books, lack of time to read, and so on. Why did Mr. Handsome want to get rid of these? Maybe his girlfriend hadn't felt like leaving the house right before the obvious incoming storm.

She pulled out a handful of crime paperbacks: Agatha Christie, Grisham, Janet Evanovich—the usual. Their spines were soft and broken—they'd probably passed through Poor Oliver's a time or two already. Some westerns from the '70s came out next, followed by a Reagan biography.

She worked quietly for a few moments, falling to a rhythm of assessing and categorizing. It surprised her when the man spoke—usually customers went searching the shelves while she tallied their credit. At least he was good looking if he did become the next lingerer.

"I know some of those paperbacks might be duplicates of what you have or might not sell. If you don't want them, I'd be happy to take them to Goodwill."

Melanie met his stare with one of her own, and the smile she gave patrons every day—cute, but not flirtatious. "Thank you. I'll be sure to return what we don't have shelf room for."

He seemed to get the picture, but he continued talking. "Is this place named after *Oliver Twist?*"

If I had a nickel. Melanie kept the friendly smile plastered on her face. "No, actually. Oliver was the name of the man who built the building back in 1890."

"Why Poor Oliver's, then?"

This guy couldn't be local. "He spent every last penny he had building this structure, which is connected to the two other shops to the...." She paused, finding her directions. "To the east."

Melanie dug back into the bag. At the bottom were three books that looked as though they had identical spines. Melanie pulled them out and turned them over to get a better look. Her heart did a double thud in her chest. Fine gold scrollwork adorned part of the spines, and on a background of red, gold lettering announced Wilkie Collins' *The Woman in White* in three volumes. She stroked the fine spines carefully, as though they might crumble under her fingers. These books had been sitting under a pile of throwaway paperbacks and were nearly ruined in the rain. Her brain didn't know where to land.

The man broke into her thoughts. "That set I'd like to ask about. I've heard you deal in rare books, as well?"

Melanie nodded. She had been saving for a set like this, even a set half as nice as this, for years now. Everything about the Victorian era intrigued her, but the books of the period were the most interesting in every genre and category: mystery, romance, horror, sensation, literary fiction, social commentary—even erotica. As far as she was concerned, the popular novel had direct roots in the Victorian era.

A set in this condition was so rare, so impossibly hard to find in the States, yet here it was: sitting on the counter at her store, its only protection a soaked paper bag from Braum's.

"Ah, yes. Yes, we do buy and sell rare books." And this set *belonged* in Poor Oliver's. She wanted it so suddenly and so ferociously that she imagined herself stealing it. She squashed the fantasy; she would do whatever it took ethically for that set to be hers.

"I looked it up online, and I think it's worth something, but I'm not sure how much."

A lot, that was certain. Thousands. But she couldn't let him see the raw happiness that was bubbling up her throat. She wondered how quickly she could get it through the proper channels, and then somehow let it sit on her rare-but-out-of-sight shelf upstairs until she could afford to buy it for herself.

She found her voice. "I'm certified through the Antiquarian Booksellers' Association of America—ABAA to you—to price this book, so I'm glad you came here instead of dropping everything at Goodwill; however, I cannot both appraise the book and sell it. You'll need to have it professionally appraised elsewhere before I can sell it."

"Oh," he said, mulling it over. It made sense. In the real estate business, the one doing the appraising certainly wasn't the one doing the buying or the selling. With something worth as much money as a house or a condo, that was to be expected, but books? Something must've shown on his face because the attractive bookseller was looking at him the way he expected a kindergarten teacher must look at her rowdy class. Or, better yet, the way a librarian must look at giggling children breaking the hush of the library. He almost couldn't stop the grin that wanted to grow on his face.

"I hope that's not an inconvenience for you," she said primly, which brought the smile fully to his lips.

"No, not at all," he said, finding his voice amidst the entertaining images in his mind that now involved ruffling the librarian's topknot. Just how many pins did she use to keep her hair looking that adorably mussed? "Just didn't expect something like that for books."

She started to put her hands on her hips, and Samuel thought, *Oh, here we go, full librarian status*, but then she dropped her hands, shaking herself as though she'd come out of a daydream.

"Most people don't," she said, matter-of-factly. "Can you come back tomorrow? And when you have the appraisal? I'll need to research this a bit more and we will have to talk about how Poor Oliver's goes about listing rar—er—older books, Mr...?"

He held out his hand, "Please, call me Samuel. It sounds much better than Mr. Reid."

It sounded like *Sam-yull*, some vestige of an accent he'd probably never had, but that his name still retained and it suited him well. The built frame, the muscular arms, the wavy hair, sharp jawline, and smart eyes were made for a name like that. She took his hand, and he warmly squeezed hers. "Samuel."

And then he smiled again. Not the upturned corners that strangers give each other when they catch the other looking their way for a moment too long, but a real smile that showed his teeth and touched his eyes, crinkling them at the corners. Or were those crow's feet? He was older than her—surely over forty—but it was hard to tell with men. It wasn't the same mischievous smile he'd had a moment ago. No, this one had a touch of heat in it.

She smiled back, feeling the seed of some hope sprout within her. Whether that was the man or the books, she wasn't sure yet. "I'm Melanie Montgomery."

Samuel leaned on the counter. "Can I buy you a drink after you close? Coffee if you don't drink? Seems the least I could do after being in your hair for the last hour or so."

Her heart dropped. This was the path to disappointment. Leaving for coffee, and then what? Going to his place? The mere thought of leaving home, let alone being so far from the shop, sent her into panic mode. Suddenly, his nearness made her nervous. She was good with small talk until she wasn't, and then her brain shut off and her worries showed up. Unless it was Anna Jane or Paul or her family, she hadn't let anyone *in* in forever.

Since before the fire.

She tried to cover her ballooning anxiety with humor, pointing a thumb over her shoulder at the coffee bar. "I'm over-caffeinated as it is." Civil, joking, nothing too flirtatious. Melanie returned to the ledger. Now, had she written 'love' or 'loathe' in that previous title? She needed to be more careful. She focused on deciphering her own handwriting to try and calm the nerves shooting through her belly. Any moment, they'd crawl up and out her throat, she knew it.

"That's not what I…"

"I know what you meant, and I know what I mean," she managed to get out, sounding much meaner than she meant it. She gripped the ledger in tight fists. *Oh, God, please just leave; please just come back tomorrow. I am not going to have a panic attack in front of a stranger.*

He looked lost for words, the playful smile gone. Melanie felt a hitch in her chest that didn't have anything to do with thoughts about leaving Poor Oliver's. She opened her mouth to say she was teasing when his smile came back, though it didn't make the dark circles under his eyes disappear. Was this guy desperate or just being nice? As much as she loved talking to people, this felt different, and she was floundering.

"How about I just come back when the book is appraised

like you said I should?"

"Samuel…" No, that sounded too familiar now that she had offended him. "Mr. Reid, I'm sorry. It's just been a long day, and I've got to start my own research on this set while it's being appraised."

"Not something a drink and venting to a stranger could help?"

The thought of leaving while it was still raining to have coffee with a stranger who didn't know her from Eve, well, it evaporated the moment of temptation. Hot humiliation began spreading over her collarbone—and in front of this good looking stranger, too.

"I'm sorry; I'm swamped this evening." *And I have to curl up in a ball and cry when you leave. Please, leave, please go. Go, go, go!*

His look of confusion gave her gnawing insides more fuel. "I'm sorry if I've offended you. I'll come back with my appraisal."

"Thank you." She offered a sweating hand, which he shook with a quick goodbye when she didn't look him in the eyes. Tears swelling, she watched his retreating figure disappear into the darkness outside the front doors. She hugged herself and wondered, just for a moment, what it would be like to follow him into the world beyond.

But it was too much. She grabbed a short stack of books and ran for the stairs. She couldn't move fast enough to beat the tears which mingled with the flush on her cheeks.

Chapter 5

Why had he decided to walk to the bookstore? As much for the exercise as to clear his head, he supposed, now that he was standing on the wet sidewalk with Melanie Montgomery in his head. He'd been used to walking in the big cities, so while his feet knew the drill, his eyes took in the surroundings. He hadn't walked these streets in twenty years now. It made him feel old.

He'd been lucky to make it into the store without ruining his first sale. Was he that bumbling fourteen-year-old again, yet to be shaped by his father's workaholic mentality and his grandfather's business savvy?

Confirmation came not a minute later from his footwear. He hadn't realized he'd left his house slippers on until they squished unceremoniously on the tile floor. Samuel looked down. Water soaked him halfway up his calves.

He'd clearly lost his mind.

But he'd worked in worse conditions, he reminded himself. Real estate only sold itself when the buyer was overeager. He was here to make a sale and make a sale he would. He raked a hand through his hair and shook some of the water from it.

He had felt eyes on him the moment he walked in, but couldn't see the person they belonged to. Used bookstores weren't high on his list of places to visit, but he liked the look of this one. The last one he'd been in was in Colorado, searching for a cookbook to pass the time in Aspen. The place was tucked away in a mountain town where businesses operated out of historic buildings from the 1850s. Whoever ran this one in Warren, Kansas had created an atmosphere that was cozy and inviting. They had a knack for organized chaos—books appeared haphazardly piled next to tall bookcases, but when he got a closer look, he found purpose in the stack, whether it be title, author, or common theme. It was a sign of a smartly run business, and he appreciated the efficiency.

The building was hushed, and the white noise from the rain was pleasant. It smelled like coffee and books, two scents that went well together. If he hadn't been so busy trying to keep the books from getting wet—in his loafers, nonetheless! Who the hell managed to leave the house with them on and not notice? He shook his head. He should have looked at the hours posted outside. If he was too close to closing, whomever looked at the rare books might want to rush him out. At least he'd put the rare books in the bottom of the bag like his grandfather had told him to. Thank God for that, if nothing else.

His first vision of her was of a woman emerging from the shelves. It was as though she had sprouted from them, rising from among the millions of pages of old binding, new paper and old, and covers in a thousand varieties. He had seen beautiful women before, and knew that he would again, but there was something different about this woman.

The more he studied her, the more he saw. Dark hair and light skin that looked like it would tan a beautiful golden brown if she ever saw the sun. She stood there in her dark skinny jeans and rose-colored t-shirt completely unaware of how lovely she looked. As she shifted, her hair fell in front of her face. She pushed it out of the way in annoyance, and it made him smile. She reminded him of a girl who'd been in his Science Fiction and Fantasy 610 course in college, the one who sat at the front of the class and answered all the questions the teacher asked, and all he could see was the back of her head. It couldn't be the same girl, but her sweep of hair stirred his memory just the same.

Maybe being in town a few weeks wasn't going to be such a drag after all. His meeting with the bookstore girl had started off sliding straight to first-date territory.

Things went downhill from there, though. Samuel was used to Chelsea and her take-no-bs work mentality which gave way to her 'treat me like a princess as soon as five rolls around' attitude once she was off the clock.

This woman clearly didn't want to be treated like a princess. He'd only wanted to help her get the book carts out of the storm.

But he'd seen the resistance in her caramel tinted eyes when he'd pressed about getting a drink.

He'd watched the red creep over her neck and up her face.

He'd seen the tears well in those deep eyes, blinked away by her professionalism.

But why? Had someone hurt her, frightened her, and made her cautious and untrusting of others? Pretty or not, a woman didn't deserve that kind of treatment.

And now his walk home was slower, more measured than the

brisk pace he'd set for himself on the way into the bookstore. He had a feeling it was going to rain again before too long, but he couldn't motivate himself to walk much faster. He didn't remember this in college. In fact, he didn't remember much from college at all. The stress of business school, the all-nighters spent studying, it had all melted into the clouds of memory, softening around the edges and making him forget how stressful it had all been. The present vision of Melanie as The Girl at the Bookstore on College Heights Road was the only thing that seemed to be in focus.

He felt out of place under large, mature trees. They intimidated him in a way that the tall buildings and the rush of the crowds in Tokyo and Brisbane hadn't. He'd thought he belonged there in his sharp suits and slick Italian shoes. This was a place for jeans and t-shirts. The only time you wore a suit was to your wedding and your funeral.

And now here he was wandering down a sidewalk lined with trees four times his age without a skyscraper in sight. His paper bag full of used books was probably still dripping on the counter at Poor Oliver's. He couldn't remember the last book he'd read. Maybe *You Are a Badass* from a few years before? He wasn't even certain he'd finished it.

Half a block later, he took off his soggy loafers and pitched them in a trashcan at the park near his grandparents' house. His soft feet didn't care for the concrete sidewalk, but he had other things on his mind.

If he *was* going through some early midlife crisis, he was glad no one from back north was here to see it happen. David would laugh at him, and Chelsea would offer to take him shopping for a new pair of Salvatore Ferragamos. They'd both tried to call him, and he hadn't answered. It was too much right now. What could you say to the people you'd worked with for fifteen years? How did you tell them the bottom fell out of your life and you had to walk away? What could you say when everything that mattered suddenly didn't any longer? On top of all that, had he just been rejected?

It was too late now, though. He wanted to know more about Melanie Montgomery. He wanted to know what had put that wariness in her eyes, that guarded tenseness in her frame. And he knew just the people to ask.

Chapter 6

She was an idiot.

When she locked up that night, she paused and stood on her favorite rug by the checkout counter to listen and watch. As her eyes adjusted to the half darkness, cut only by the yellow street lights outside, the bookshelves looked back at her—silent sentinels stationed throughout the one huge room—her business, her home, her place of worship. She couldn't make out individual titles, but metallic lettering glinted and faint light bounced off protective coverings of hardbacks and shiny paperbacks.

She couldn't hear much from where she stood. The occasional car going by was muted by thick glass, the air conditioning was on low, and the dehumidifier was distant white noise, like waves on the beach from the grassy edge of the sand.

"What should I do?" she asked. She thought to ask the cats, then remembered they weren't there to ask anymore.

She couldn't help it if she daydreamed of magic, though.

If sometimes, when she was alone, like now, she wished for more than what was within these walls. It wasn't silly, she reasoned, to sometimes pretend that magic existed, that someday a wizard would accidentally donate his spell book to Poor Oliver's, that she could peer inside and find the spell that would let her leave without so much as a second thought. Or that a knight would rush though the doors and announce that he had found a way to break her curse.

But the books only sat there and watched silently, speaking their secrets to each other. If they answered, she did not hear them.

Perhaps that was what she should do—nothing. She was fine with the way her life was right now; in fact, she was happy. No crisis had upended her life lately, she was making excellent money, the first stage of renovations to her upstairs living area had wrapped up wonderfully. Her health was also good. She had nothing to complain about, so why should she pursue some man who might end up being a jerk after a few dates or who might only want to take her on a few dates and waste her time?

The books still said nothing, but she could feel them watching. They had seen so much, these used books, their covers, their pages, held by millions of people. Each book she put on a shelf meant that she, too, had touched those hands through time and history.

Melanie wandered upstairs, noting again that the stairs and banisters needed to be refinished. It soothed her to think that with so much work to do around here, there was really no need to leave.

But, she knew that thought wasn't healthy. Then again, PTSD with a side of agoraphobia and anxiety wasn't exactly healthy either.

She wandered through her small kitchen to the bathroom to get ready for bed. Once there, she stared at the bottles of medication in her small bathroom instead of washing her face. Zoloft, Diazepam, Klonopin, some Kava that didn't do anything. Pills she hadn't taken in a few months now. She'd just gotten busy, she justified, and she hadn't needed to leave. She got more done when the groceries were delivered and when Paul brought her extra delicious food on the regular.

Can I buy you a cup of coffee?

Who said no to such a simple request? And what idiot responded like she didn't care?

Handsome strangers weren't uncommon. Watching people pass by the windows every day, she saw dozens of handsome faces. But when did a handsome face, who actually came in, express interest in *her*? Sure, old men flirted, and the why-not-give-it-a-try women slipped her their number on merchant copy receipts occasionally, but she'd never given them a second thought, never returned any flirtations, never called any of the numbers scribbled on receipts and signed with hearts.

Paul and a few other men had seemed promising in her college days, but they had disappointed each other and gone their separate ways. Otherwise…she had her books.

And that collection! She'd spent an hour poring over Abe Books after she closed up only to determine that it was indeed worth every penny of four grand. She hated the idea that someone might snatch it up before she was able to rightfully afford such a rare and beautiful set. Would Samuel come back the next day to talk pricing? He had promised, but he didn't seem like the book type—and she had practically shooed him out. But where had he found something so valuable?

She picked up the bottle of Zoloft and scanned its label as though she hadn't seen it a hundred times already, considering whether she wanted to start taking it again. She heard her psychiatrist's voice in her head much more clearly this time.

"Why aren't you taking your Zoloft? I thought it helped you."

"It did. I just didn't want to get addicted to everything I was taking."

"These medicines are very safe when used correctly. Were you using them like you were supposed to?"

"Yes, of course."

"And you felt better on them?"

"Yeah."

"Then why are you punishing yourself by not taking them? I would not steer you wrong. I want you to feel better, too."

Melanie set the bottle down. It'd been hell weaning off all the meds last time, and to restart all that? To go back to the beginning and find the cocktail that worked, to talk again about the things that brought the demons out? No, she wasn't ready. There was always tomorrow.

Chapter 7

Melanie Montgomery, slinger of books. He got the distinct feeling that she didn't know just how fine her ass looked in those jeans. What did she do when she wasn't perusing pages? Did she curl up with a glass of whiskey and a book? Or did she let her hair down and hit one of the bars, perhaps dancing to a local band?

He wanted to know. There was something about the casual way she carried herself, the way he'd felt her eyes on him the moment he'd walked in. She had the spark of warm interest in her eyes, something the women he'd met in Vancouver and abroad hadn't had. The women he worked with were worried about the sale, worried about their image, didn't have time to even look at him unless they needed something. Melanie Montgomery had a brain that he already admired.

The day after he went to Poor Oliver's, he drove to the bookstore Melanie sent him to. Second Day Books didn't have the charm of the place in Warren, and the guy manning the front certainly wasn't as nice to look at as Melanie. But Samuel was promised an appraisal in what seemed like a reasonable amount of time.

Being back in Warren after so long had seemed claustrophobic at first, but Samuel felt relaxed on his drive to and from Second Day Books. The rolling Flint Hills and their waving grasses soothed him instead of inciting fear of permanency. There was still something missing, though. Could Melanie Montgomery be the missing piece to that puzzle?

Samuel called Chloe when he got back, settling onto his grandparents' front porch with a sigh. He didn't know if he'd ever get used to 'sitting around.' Chloe was surprised to hear that he was in town.

"I thought you were done with any town under a population of half a million," she laughed.

"Just needed a change of scenery," he grumbled. Ice melted in his two fingers of whiskey. The air hung heavy that evening, but he found he'd missed watching the sun set through the trees.

"Well, we'll have to get some of us together if you have time while you're here. John and Sara stayed in town. They have a baby now."

"Look at us go. Business and marketing department geniuses."

"At least one of us went big time." Chloe's remark was genuine.

"Yeah, well. What about you? You and Erica still together?"

"God, don't get me started on that bitch. I'm happily single. Send the women my way."

"Just don't take mine."

He could feel the interest in her voice immediately. "Oh?

36

What's this? Did the playboy finally find someone?"

"I wouldn't say that, but…" He launched into his story.

When he finished, Chloe was thoughtful. "I mean, everyone knows Poor Oliver's. It's a staple downtown. If that's the dark-haired chick who's in there all the time, then she's also the owner. She's had the place for a while. I know her best friend better, though." Whom Chloe had known *much* better. The thought sent a pang straight through her heart, one she tried to squash down as soon as she felt it.

"She owns it?"

"Literally what I just said," she said more coolly than she intended. Damn Reid for dredging up memories he didn't know he was unearthing.

"Know anyone else who might know her?"

He heard the laugh track for a sitcom in the background. "AJ over at the Walnut Café knows her well. That place is basically across the street from Poor Oliver's. And they have kickass potato salad."

"I'll pass on the potato salad, but thanks. I'll see what he knows."

"She," Chloe corrected.

"Sorry, she," Samuel replied. Then, feeling the honesty well up within him, "She's very guarded. I like her, Chloe, as a person. I don't want to frighten her."

Chloe didn't speak for a beat, and he wondered what she knew. "Be a friend to her, Sam. Something happened a few years ago, but I'll let her tell you. I'm not one for gossip."

Armed with his information—not that it was much—Samuel spent the rest of the night researching the books from his grandfather's attic.

This sudden immersion into the world of books unsettled

him. He'd been more of a reader before real estate took over his life. Hell, he'd barely had time for food and the gym between clients the last few years. Forget about having a girlfriend. Sure, there'd been girls, but none of them stuck around when they realized what kind of schedule he had and how much time he had for them—which was approximately zero. The books then had been more of the *Win Friends and Influence People* type, but he could appreciate a page-turner, could appreciate the work that had gone into creating a world for the reader, whether fiction or nonfiction. He'd been as into *Lord of the Rings* as the other brains in middle school.

He pushed his chair back from the desk. God, he hadn't thought about reading in years. He grinned as he remembered reading his mom's worn copies of King novels under a blanket with a flashlight late into the night. She had to have known he was reading them, but she never scolded her twelve-year-old for reading something that was probably darker than anything a twelve-year-old had any right to know.

Melanie's dark eyes and the pleasant memories of days long gone kept following him. He wondered just what it might take to get her to loosen that knot of hair that sat so neatly on top of her head, what it would take to get her laughing, whether she liked *Lord of the Rings*. He admired a girl with a good sense of humor, and her sarcasm hadn't been lost on him. Even if it took a bit of teasing to bring it out, he had a feeling it'd be worth it. And appraisal or no, he thought tomorrow would be a good day for another visit.

Chapter 8

The next morning, Melanie spent more time than she cared to admit standing in front of her full-length mirror picking at the pile of hair on her head and the mascara on her eyelashes. She found her nicest dark jeans but stuck with the usual literary t-shirt, tied at the hip to reveal just a hint of skin. Well, and there was the lacy bra that showed just the tiniest bit through her shirt. And the heart outline with the word 'BOOKS' inside settled nicely over her left breast. Hell, she ran the place, she could wear whatever she wanted. She was not, *not*, dressing up for Samuel Reid, who might be coming by. She knew approximately how quickly James Young worked, and it wasn't out of the question for the appraisal to be finished today.

She puttered around upstairs after completing her extended morning ritual. She stared out over her space, trying to soothe herself. What if Samuel wasn't actually flirting? Then getting all dolled up—which she swore to herself wasn't for him—would be for nothing. It wasn't for nothing, though—it was for her. Wasn't it? She didn't want to appear desperate…

Melanie took a deep breath. "You're fine. You're fine," she chanted.

She wandered from her living area to the delayed pick up and shipping shelves. It was an honor to share space with these rare and less handled books. Customers weren't allowed in the thousand square feet above the main store. About half of it was her studio apartment. The rest was bookshelves and antique storage. The windows looked over the small shopping district and to the trees and hills beyond. Living where you worked, when you loved where you worked, was the epitome of awesome.

She had what she needed here—a European style fridge, stove, and microwave oven in the kitchen, a tiny bathroom off the kitchen. They had managed to squeeze in the clawfoot tub next to the reclaimed twenties-style sink and a toilet. Next to the bathroom was a linen closet and laundry room that boasted the most modern of her appliances: a miniature high efficiency washer and dryer, which she'd bought of necessity after customers asked about strange rumbling sounds coming from upstairs. The table and two chairs in the kitchen served as an eating and preparation space, and a bedroom beyond was sized to serve its purpose. She didn't spend much time there. It was better, and more interesting, to sleep in the various nooks and crannies created by the bookshelves upstairs. It was like her secret garden.

She loved her nest. It was cozy and, like her store below, full of books. What else did she need? She took another deep breath and smiled. Yes, she was happy here.

Feeling calmer, she slipped into her Birkenstocks and headed downstairs.

At a few 'til nine, she let Paul in the back door. He took one look at her and his eyebrows shot up. He whistled appreciatively.

Melanie playfully tapped him on the arm and took the paper bag from him. It smelled like a scone or a muffin. Blueberry. Her mouth watered. "Don't judge me. I can wear whatever I want."

Paul brushed past her, laughing. "Who's the lucky guy?"

Melanie pretended to trip him. "Punk. It's a secret."

He dodged her and laughed. "It's me, isn't it?"

"Oh, yes, Paul, it's you all right." She chuckled and headed toward the front register. "Thanks for the food, though, darling."

"Also, I need a favor. Just a tiny one."

"Okay?" Melanie paused her trek to assess a stack of the *Harry Potter* series in the young adult section. The spiral was off, as though someone had bumped into the display. She set her breakfast down to fix it properly.

"They need a hand unloading the food truck next door."

"And?" Finished, Melanie eyed another stack of young adult reads that needed to be adjusted. She smiled at each spine as she slid the books into their proper place. Yes, that looked great.

"You can leave for ten minutes and help me."

Melanie shot him a look. She refused to consider it. Paul looked so hopeful; she hated to crush his good cheer. "No."

Paul was immediately animated. "But, it shares a wall with this building! It's practically the same place. Same bricks and everything. You barely have to go outside."

Melanie continued stacking, trying to look unperturbed. It was better not to think about going outside. Outside was the place she had gone when the fire happened. Outside was where she had been when she hadn't been there to save the cats. Outside was bad. But if she let on to how much it bothered her, Paul would only pester her more. "I think I appreciate what you're trying to do here, but today is not the day."

"Oh, come on!" Paul said lightheartedly. He set a gentle hand on the small of her back and the other at her elbow, trying to steer her toward the back door. That led outside. To the street. "You can put the 'Back in 10 Minutes' sign on the door and everything."

"Um, no!" Melanie dug her heels in and spun away. "Definitely not, but thanks for playing."

He reached for her elbow again, this time in full playing mode, but Melanie wasn't playing. And, she'd spent too long on her hair and mascara to go unload a truck. She wasn't going to mess her hair and makeup up for some fool's errand and Paul's unsolicited attempt to help. She didn't want to leave, and that was final.

"I said no, you jerk!" Melanie swung a fist at him and caught him squarely in the shoulder.

"Ow!"

"That'll teach you," she said.

"Your knuckles are bony," Paul said, rubbing his shoulder.

"Good for cracking skulls and warding off unwanted advances," she replied, only half teasing. Paul was one of the only people who knew about her *situation*, and sometimes he considered himself a therapist, trying to get her outside when he thought it'd be easier for her. Some days she could appreciate his misguided helpfulness, but today she was not in the mood.

Chapter 9

S he was flirting with an attractive boy about her age when Samuel entered the store. That he hadn't considered that she might have a boyfriend, or a husband for that matter, unsettled him.

He knew he was inviting trouble by coming back so early, but he'd brought another book, and he was itching to learn more about Melanie Montgomery.

Samuel scanned the building. From a real estate perspective, this place was gold. It sat on a busy corner of the historic shopping district, and there had to be original architecture under those dropped ceiling tiles. Someone had probably lost their mind in the '80s and covered it all up. He thought about his style choices in the '80s and decided that they may have all lost their minds back then.

He'd spent the night trying to get her out of his head. That soft, pale face and curtain of dark hair. He could only imagine so much what her hands felt like before he had to find out for himself. Not that he'd expected Chloe to know much about her, but her cryptic tip added to the mystery and to his desire to get a better picture of her.

It wasn't that he needed a distraction, but he really needed a distraction.

Thank God he had the sense to wear actual shoes this time with his jeans and black Calvin Klein t-shirt. He'd brought her coffee and another book, although he wasn't certain he'd give it up just yet. He'd been astounded at how much people paid for books. He'd felt almost sick touching the copy of *The Picture of Dorian Gray* with his bare hands.

When he looked up from his contemplations, there was a scuffle happening between Melanie and the guy. Hadn't he seen that guy in the area yesterday? Was he stalking her? Samuel strode toward them. Stranger or not, the guy was hassling Melanie, and he wasn't going to stand for it. "Hey, asshole, leave her alone."

The two sprang apart and turned to look at him as though he'd just shot a gun in a closed space.

"I don't know what you're bothering her about, but you need to stop."

Melanie's eyes were spitting fire when they met his. Oh, she was sexy when she was upset. And that full pout on her lips… he had to get those smoldering eyes alone.

"You don't have to put up with him. I can haul him out of here if you want."

Melanie's eyes shone, but not with tears. It looked like laughter. At least the guy had the sense to be mortified. He opened his mouth to say something, but Samuel stopped him with a pointed finger.

"Yes, you," Samuel said. "Quit badgering her."

The guy looked down at Melanie, who stood a full head

shorter than him. "Am I badgering you?"

Melanie socked the guy in the arm again. "Yes, but I know your mother, and if I tell her you're being a pest, she'll take you over her knee and spank you into next week."

Samuel felt as though he'd missed something vital. "Um…" he floundered.

"Samuel, this is Paul. Paul, Samuel," Melanie offered. Then, to Paul, "The rare books I mentioned."

Samuel opened his mouth to protest the change of subject, but his brain hadn't caught up and Melanie's smile had turned into a grin so sexy he'd forgotten what he'd come over there for in the first place.

"Paul's one of my best friends." She pinched Paul, who yelped. "He was just being a jackass, like usual."

"Sorry, man. Mel, I'm gonna go next door for a bit. No harm, no foul, dude." Paul held his hands up to Samuel and then disappeared out the back door.

"That's not your boyfriend," Samuel stated.

"He's my best friend." Melanie was flushed and stray hairs had escaped from her cute updo to crowd around her face. He wanted to bury his hands in it, but this was now the second time he'd embarrassed himself in front of her.

Oh, yes, that blush of pink looked good on her. "What was he bothering you about?"

Melanie brushed something from her right breast that he couldn't see. "He thinks I should get out more. In the form of unloading the food truck next door. Nice try, really, but I'm not feeling like doing more manual labor than lifting books for the next eight hours."

She took the coffee he offered and eyed the book under his arm. "What's that?"

"Something else you might be interested in."

He watched her eyes shift over him—not just the book. And he noticed that she looked especially nice today. Her dark jeans hugged every curve of her hips and legs. They were turned up just at her ankles, revealing more of that creamy skin he wanted to get his mouth on, and ended with some very worn, very cute Birkenstocks. A hint of skin at her hip teased him again. He wondered what she would do with his mouth on that spot, whether it was a pleasurable tickle that made her groan or if it would make her giggle and squirm. He didn't mind wrestling with a willing participant.

When he looked up finally, he swore she was breathing a tad harder than she had been. The wary look was in her eyes again, but he also saw interest and curiosity. He wasn't one to assume, though. Maybe it was for the book.

"Um...so," she recovered with a deep breath and a sweet, professional smile. "Books."

Her eyes were wide, cautious. God, she was pretty. Surely someone admired her dark hair and chocolate eyes. Someone must be giving those lips of hers the attention they deserved. If not....well, being back in Kansas might not be so bad after all.

He handed her the book. "I did some research on this one before I brought it in. It looks valuable, but I don't know anything about editions and all that. There's a huge range of pricing online. I don't know how you do it."

She flipped the cover open, flipped delicately through several pages, and let out a gasp that he couldn't read. When she looked up, those big eyes were full of mist. "Where are you finding all these books?"

Samuel recognized the look in her eyes. Greed wasn't the

name for it, no. This woman wasn't greedy, but she was *wanting*.

But did she want more than books?

He very much wanted to find out.

Chapter 10

She was certain it was a first printing of *Dorian Gray*. The embossed tan and gray cover ticked several important rare book boxes. But when she opened the book, she could only stare in a daze at the curling leaf design near the title on the interior page above the printer's mark for Ward, Lock, and Company. 'Ultra rare' didn't approach what this book appeared to be.

When Samuel didn't answer immediately, she looked up and caught him watching her. Not in an uncomfortable way, just a curious way. For as much as she'd messed up the day before, he didn't seem upset with her. "I'm sorry. I don't mean to pry. We just don't get books like these in. Ever really. I mean, I—we—deal in rare books every day, but books like this don't just walk in. And now you've brought by multiples in two days."

Samuel shrugged, a gesture that drew her attention to his strong arms and shoulders. The thought of him righting that book cart again made her feel a little hot—for a reason beyond embarrassment. "I don't know anything about them really. My grandparents like to go to estate sales. They've an eye for collectibles, especially antiques."

Melanie hummed her assent. That wasn't atypical. Books handed down through the generations were popular, too. Garage sales. Dumpsters, even. "I'm surprised I haven't seen them in here. What's their last name?"

"Reid, like me," he said with a smile that left her a bit weak in the knees. Surely he knew how charming he was.

"Oh," she managed to squeak out. "No Reids that I've seen."

"So how does this work?" he asked.

His question caught her off guard. She was imagining what it might be like to run her hands through that hair of his. "Hmm?"

"The books. How does the sale of rare books work? I know you said I have to get them appraised before you can sell them. Do you do appraisals too?"

"Oh," she said stupidly. She felt like all the sense she'd ever had had just left her head. "Well."

And then he was smiling at her. Melanie felt the slow, warm pull from his gaze deep in her belly, and she had to catch her breath. He looked like the stuff dreams were made of, like Heathcliff with a heart of gold and Mr. Darcy with a dash of Rhett Butler rolled into one package. She thought for a moment that he might lean in to kiss her, but she took a step back and the spell broke. She was simply standing in a bookshop—*her* bookshop—with a book that was probably worth thousands of dollars, talking to a man who had no idea what a treasure he had.

"Well," she said again, finding her composure and putting a bit more distance between herself and the handsome Samuel Reid. "You bring me the appraisal from a reputable third-party.

I do my own research on the books thoroughly to corroborate the appraisal, then set them up both on the store website as well as the international website—Morrison's, if you've heard of them."

She was sure he hadn't, but continued, "Yes, I do appraisals, but you're welcome to keep getting appraisals from James Young, then bring the books here. It keeps the paperwork nicely in order when I have an appraisal from someone I know."

Well, *know* was a relative term. She *knew* James Young was an ABAA bookseller. She *knew* James Young had unceremoniously grabbed her ass the last time she'd attended an outside ABAA event. She *knew* James Young hadn't been the least bit sorry for the aforementioned grabbing.

"What's my commission?" These were terms he understood well. From the insanity which was the real estate world, he felt much more comfortable in this low stakes situation with a book. The stakes were higher with Melanie, as far as he was concerned.

"Forty percent, minus the stocking fee."

"There's a stocking fee? For you to hold a book on your shelf? Why didn't you mention that with the other set I brought in?"

"It's five dollars." She waved her hand dismissively. "A bargain in the insurance world. I'll hold both the set and this one for that once they're appraised."

"Oh," he smiled again, and she almost said to forget the stocking fee, just please keep smiling. "That's fine then."

"I do the legwork," she said, "so you're getting a lot for that five-dollar shelf fee."

"I feel like I'm getting quite a lot just by standing here talking to you," he said, more to see how she would react. She was no fool, but he wanted to tease her, watch her flutter.

"Oh? Hmm," she said, suddenly feeling like he was standing very close.

And then he did step closer and set his hand over hers, clasping the book tightly. "Maybe you could come see my grandparents' house sometime. I mean, for the books. My grandfather's got a thousand books in that attic, and I have no idea what to do with them. Things might move along more quickly that way."

For the books or for them? Her throat wanted to close up around his words, like they were stuck in her own throat, and she couldn't swallow them or get them to come out. She began to imagine walking out of the store to go to a stranger's house—no. She shut down the thought. She was not ending this day the same as yesterday.

But for books? Couldn't she do that? It seemed like she could...or should.

"I don't leave much," she said. That was the truth. Sort of. It had started as simply working overtime to build everything back up after the fire, and sleeping near the shelves eased the recurring nightmares. Then, she'd been offered the business because the owners wanted to retire. They couldn't handle rebuilding, and she was young and eager. She sold her car to help pay for the building. Basically everything was in walking distance. She'd really meant to buy another car at some point, but...it just hadn't happened. She'd spent more and more time at the bookstore, shutting out anything *outside*. The fire had taken half her store and both the cats, and she didn't like thinking about it.

"I get it; you're busy," he said with that slow smile again.

Good God, this man was truly flirting with her, wasn't he? That thought jarred loose her typically circular thoughts about avoiding anything that meant going out. It threw a wrench in her system. She didn't know if she liked that yet or not. "No. I mean yes, I am busy, but not like that. I just…" Could she say it? No. "I just prefer to stay in." She sounded high maintenance, and he would quickly figure out that he didn't want any of that around.

And yet he seemed to take it in stride. "Just a thought," he replied. He seemed to take her statement as a vague notion that she was a homebody. "Can I take you to dinner tonight? I do want to learn more about the books I'm bringing in, and I hate to take up your time here—I understand there are other customers who need you."

Who *needed* her. The phrase shot right through like every third word that came out of his mouth. Did he flirt like this with everyone? "I don't leave much," she repeated. Here she was, making a total ass of herself. *Good God, woman, pull yourself together. You are a professional. Act like one.*

"Well, I have no qualms about bringing food *to* you," he said.

Relief and reassurance washed over her, a solution to her problem that she hadn't even entertained. "That would be perfect, actually," she said. "I've got a nice table upstairs in my apartment. We could eat there, or down here once I close up."

"You live here?"

"I do," she said, and tried to gauge his reaction. She was starting to get nervous that she couldn't read him. What did he think about her living in a bookstore? Did he think it was stupid? That *she* was stupid for picking such a career? She didn't even know him and she was inviting him into her space. What was she thinking? She tried to stuff down the feelings that their conversation stirred up. All the signs were there. The heat creeping up her ghostly pale face, the erratic heartbeat, the dizziness, and the vertigo that accompanied most of her panic attacks.

"I'm sorry," she said into the brief silence. He opened his mouth to reply, but her mouth kept spilling words. "I don't really leave much at all, and I do all of my work on the rare books in the evening."

"I meant what I said. I'll bring food here." He saw the panicked animal look in her eyes again. It made him want to soothe her, to pet her hair and tell her everything was okay.

Melanie breathed an inward sigh of relief. "That would be wonderful, thank you. I promise I won't work while we're eating."

He held out a hand, and she reached out as though to shake it, but he took her fingers into his hand and squeezed them gently, an intimate and courtly gesture. It warmed her. "Tomorrow evening?" he asked. "I'll take this book in to get appraised, too. I think that James Young guy emailed me the other one. Can I forward that to the store email?"

Before she could say 'no' and think herself out of it, she quickly agreed and focused on the way his answering smile pulled at the corner of his eyes just so. A flirtation, a diversion—both would be good for her.

Chapter 11

The store felt empty when Samuel left. She'd managed to exchange numbers with him without losing her mind. And dinner in the shop? She couldn't believe her luck.

She texted her best friend asking her to come over as quickly as she could. Even if Anna Jane didn't know what to do, she would at least listen when she got there.

As she waited, she tried to quell her excitement. It was just dinner. Nothing special. Just a persistent guy who wanted to get to know her. But it didn't help that the day moved so slowly, that the times between customers stretched on forever. She watched the clock obsessively after she closed, waiting for Anna Jane to get off her shift across the street. They'd known each other for a decade now—long enough to have formed a tight friendship.

Melanie watched her friend slip in the front entrance and latch it behind her. Anna Jane knew the drill.

"Coffee?" Melanie called from the alcove on the far wall. Even in the dimmed lights, Melanie could make out Anna Jane's confident stride. Unmistakably feminine to Melanie, she knew that Anna Jane—who preferred to go by AJ sometimes—was often called a boy by those who didn't care to look any harder. AJ's long, dark hair was smoothed and up in a cute ponytail that Melanie was jealous of. She could do the messy bun, but to tame the flyaways? Forget it.

"I will die if I don't get coffee," Anna Jane replied. "We were slammed tonight. You'd think the weather would've kept everyone away, but even I had to bust my ass this evening."

"You had to work for once?" Melanie laughed, then busied herself with the espresso machine—a splurge from last year. Coffee and books. It really didn't get much better than that.

"You're funny," Anna Jane quipped as she sighed over her first sip. "And yes. I sent Paul home early during a lull. We always get a rush when I do that."

"He probably went to see Brenna after that."

Anna Jane peeked at a display of kid books that she assumed Melanie had artfully arranged. Everything from the shelves to the merch displays looked great, and Melanie's eye for orderly disorder was everywhere. She was proud of her friend, for the business she'd grown, and where it would go in the future. "Or what's-her-name."

"Jenny?" Melanie wondered.

"I don't know. Flavor of the month. That poor kid needs to figure out what he wants."

They sipped and conversed while Melanie puttered around cleaning and organizing. Anna Jane told her about the goings on across the street at the Walnut Café and around town in a way that didn't make Melanie feel like she was missing out on

55

anything. She appreciated and enjoyed her friend's company.

"Spill the tea," Anna Jane finally said, setting her coffee down, her eyes bright and sparkling with curiosity.

Melanie thrust a dust broom at her friend. "Sweep with me and I'll tell you."

Anna Jane took the broom and started weaving over the wood floor between the shelves. Melanie was close behind to sweep the far side that Anna Jane couldn't reach.

"His name's Samuel," Melanie said as they reached the second row. The sparse light from the street outside combined with the dim lights inside scattered shadows across the floor.

"And?" The 'schk-schk' sound of the brooms broke the silence before Melanie answered.

"He's really nice," she finally said. How could she say what it meant to her that he would bring dinner to the shop, even if he didn't know why she wanted it there? Anna Jane would understand, but she still had a hard time talking about it.

"He said he'd bring dinner to me here. Tomorrow night."

That piqued Anna Jane's attention. "So, he knows?"

"No."

"Then why is he bringing food here?"

Melanie paused to take a long drink of coffee, and her eyes watered when the heat of it hit her throat. She coughed and sputtered, and Anna Jane watched with a bemused look on her face.

"Wow, sorry. Went down the wrong way."

"So?"

"So, I almost choked."

"Oh Jesus, Mel. Why is he bringing food here if he doesn't know about your thing?"

"I just told him I didn't leave much because I was busy."

"Is he dumb or just that nice?"

"I think he's just that nice. Or he's excited about the prospect of making money off rare books. He brought in an amazing Victorian set. I know you won't know it, but it's *The Woman in White*. If I had to pick a favorite from the era, that really might be it. But it's ultra rare. I don't see books like that very often."

Anna Jane chuckled and swept on, cruising around the pricing table. "You know me. Totally illiterate. I'm happy for you, though. He sounds better than Paul on first impressions. Or Juan Pablo whatever from college."

Melanie cringed. "We'll see. I sent him to James's for appraisals."

"Oh, God! You know he's a keeper if he comes back here after that guy."

"I know. I feel kind of bad now. But I'll know if he's a jerk if he says one word about liking James. I freaking hate that guy."

"You are diabolical." Anna Jane paused her sweeping again. "Listen, you know I'm not going to push you, but...."

"I know," Melanie interrupted. "I'm just going to see how this goes first. I'll tell him eventually."

"The right person won't care. Well, not *not* care. You know what I mean. They'll accept you as you are."

Melanie felt fear uncoil in her gut and slither through her insides. It said everyone cared eventually. It said everyone would want her to go outside eventually. She grabbed her coffee for another hot drink, trying to drown her thoughts. "I hope so," she finally said. *Don't hope too hard*, the snake of anxiety hissed, the thought slithering through the deepest parts of her, the parts which hoped against hope that she would find someone, someday, who stayed.

Chapter 12

The next day wasn't as hard to get through as she expected, helped along by the promise of the sale of *Dorian Gray*, offered first to Hans Delbrook, since he'd certainly snap it up. The American expat had been living in Germany for nearly thirty years—not that anyone could tell by his name—and was among her oldest customers. She had heard through the ABAA grapevine that he was on a first name basis with a handful of her colleagues as he built up his collection of rare books, so she was always happy when something came in that he'd likely purchase. No more than five minutes had passed between her emailing the private listing and his phone call to claim his intention. Everything in her gut said the appraisal would go through smoothly, and, with as quickly as James Young worked, it might even come in that day.

Once she had the appraisal in hand, it would surely be her first six figure sale, and though it wasn't complete yet, she was dizzy with elation.

She'd tell Samuel once the sale was completed to prevent potential disappointment. If she could keep it to herself that long.

They decided on takeout from Aloy Thai, which Melanie had promised was delicious. With only thirty minutes before Samuel was supposed to arrive, she bolted upstairs to frantically clean her living quarters.

She gathered armfuls of clothes and shoved them into her two laundry bins, then pushed the bins into the laundry closet. Most of those clothes were from her morning trying to figure out what the hell to wear. As it turned out, she didn't have a lot worth keeping. She had just been rotating through the same dozen t-shirts and a selection of jeans for the last five years. It was amazing Paul hadn't said anything.

In the kitchen, she shoved cereal bowls and spoons into the dishwasher and stacked her bills into a presentable pile on the table. No, that was too cluttered. She stuffed them beside the fridge and then stood back to look at the room.

She smiled at the way the kitchen's linoleum suddenly ended in hardwood, a few feet from where bookshelves sprouted up. It was like a slice of the bookstore had time-warped into her home. Paul had once offered to frame in her living area, but she liked the way rows of shelves served as her front yard of sorts. And besides, only she and Paul were ever up here. And now Samuel, this once, at least, so it wasn't like anyone regularly judged her choice of living situation.

If this sale went through, she could have the linoleum pulled up so she could run hardwood throughout the rest of the apartment. And she would find a way to stay during the renovation. There would be no fire this time, no rags left in an enclosed space to combust and send her world spiraling.

Distantly, she heard a knock on the back door. Taking a deep breath, she ran downstairs to answer it.

Samuel was there with carryout bags in his hands. The same sweet smile he had given her during their first meeting gave her heart a slight misstep again. The soft light on the back porch did nothing to conceal the handsome shape of his body. He'd worn a black t-shirt, and she openly admired how his arms held his sleeves captive.

Feeling bolstered by his smile, she took the bags from him and invited him upstairs. He went first, treading up to her space. She took a moment to appreciate his backside as he walked up the stairs. It might be a crime for a man to have an ass that nice. It looked damn good in those dark jeans.

"Watch your step at the top—it's a bit loose."

Samuel hopped over the last stair and said, "I don't want to seem like that guy, but do you need someone to fix that for you?"

"Oh, Paul will get to it eventually."

Samuel bent down and wiggled the board. "It doesn't need much, probably just a screw from the backside of the tread. I have time tomorrow."

"I don't want to bother you with—"

"It's not a bother," he interrupted. "I have the time, and I'd like to help." And he did. Very much so, he realized.

"Okay," she said, her wide eyes holding his.

She relaxed as she moved around her kitchen, setting out the food while he took in the sight of the bookcases steps away. "Is this where you keep the rare books?"

"And double copies of anything I don't want to give up. It used to be a larger apartment, but when we expanded our rare books area, I had to downsize. I'm not complaining, though. I love living in a forest of books." She felt a great happiness at that statement, and she hoped that Samuel could hear in her voice how much she did, in fact, enjoy living here.

"What do you do when you leave town?" Surely she had the rarest books locked up somewhere. That someone could just walk up here to this open space and take what they wanted made him worried for Melanie's safety even though he didn't know her—or the area, anymore, he had to admit—like he wanted to.

"Oh, I don't vacation," she said nonchalantly. "I don't mind; it's my favorite place to be. Bathroom's the first door on the right if you need to wash your hands. If you reach my bedroom, you've gone too far."

When Samuel disappeared to wash his hands, Melanie set flatware and napkins on the table with shaking hands. She had invited him up to her apartment for dinner—what was she thinking? In all the years she'd been here, she wasn't sure if anyone other than Paul and Anna Jane had come up, and here she was letting in a stranger. Sure, he was easy to talk to about books and any other silly thing, but what had possessed her to think she should do this? And why was he taking so long in the bathroom? Was he feeling uncomfortable? Did he want to leave, but he was just trying to figure out how to tell her?

The familiar clawing didn't just creep up this time. It crashed over her like the torrent of rain that had soaked her book carts. She braced her hands on the table, her vision tunneling out. No, she would not faint here, not now. She'd made it through the other meetings with him—this wasn't any different.

As he came out of the bathroom, she slipped in behind him, unable to look at his face. "My turn!" she said, trying to sound cheerful.

She shoved the door shut and gripped the sides of the sink until her knuckles turned white. She desperately fought the feelings crushing her down.

"Go away, go away, go away," she chanted quietly, but her voice couldn't slice through the hammering of her heart in her ears. She heard Samuel shifting at the table and knew she'd been in there too long. Could she just stay in there until he left? No, she had to face him.

"I don't feel well," Melanie blurted out when she came out of the bathroom.

She saw the look of reciprocal panic on his face when he looked at her, and it sent her spiraling further. Tears sprang into her eyes and she couldn't stop them.

Samuel opened his mouth to say something, but she beat him to it. "You have to go." She wasn't going to stand there and let him see her like this, to tell her she was crazy for being fine one second and a trainwreck the next.

When she set a hand on his shoulder and nudged him toward the stairs and door, he jolted as though he'd been shocked. His brain couldn't process fast enough to understand what was happening. Had she gotten some horrible text telling her a family member had died? What had happened? "Melanie, what's..." But she cut him off before he could say anything else.

"Please just leave," she sobbed, even as her heart cried for him to stay. This is what she'd been afraid of. He'd never come back now. Somewhere beneath the panic, she had to admire that for as much as he felt like a solid wall of muscle, he was allowing her, someone less than half his size, to push him quite quickly out the door.

Chapter 13

Melanie made it to the top of the stairs before her legs gave out. Determined, she crawled to the bathroom and its cool, tiled floor. She scrambled up to open the mirrored cabinet and pulled out a valium. Her stomach fluttered. It seemed like a safety net, like a cheat. But she wanted to know Samuel better.

She wanted to *try* for this handsome man who wanted to know more about books. About *her* books. About *her*. That she had probably just imploded anything between them wasn't a thought she could entertain yet. She clutched at the thought of him like a lifeline, about how his eyes really hadn't looked judgmental when she'd rushed out of the bathroom looking like *Jane Eyre's* woman in the attic. He'd opened his mouth to say something, and she'd shut him down and shoved him out. But she still had a choice. She slipped the valium into her mouth and stuck her head under the faucet for water.

She made it back to the kitchen table before her legs got wobbly again. The bags of still-hot food brought on a fresh wave of tears. God, he'd probably been trying to help her, hadn't he? He'd opened his mouth to ask what was wrong and she'd just pushed him down the stairs, wanting him gone immediately.

No.

Her desire to keep things as they were wanted him out of there. Her fear that equated change with outside. Her constant battle with memories of that horrible fire.

It wasn't her. *She* wanted him there—and acknowledging that loosened something in her.

There was a soft knock on the back door.

Her heart lurched. He was waiting out there.

The knocking persisted.

It finally quieted. The door opened. Oh, God! Why hadn't she locked it?

His voice floated up the stairs. "Melanie?"

She was still frozen at the kitchen table when he appeared at the top of the stairs. His dark hair was tousled, like he'd been running his hands through it. When he ran a hand over the stubble that was just becoming a beard on his tanned jawline, she saw the concern on his face that was etched there just as surely as there was smeared mascara under her eyes.

"What happened?" he asked.

Fresh tears burned her eyes."Why did you come back?"

He reached for her then, and her automatic response was to reach for him in return. He pulled her into a hug that felt so kind, she burst into tears.

"Shhhhh, I'm not going to leave you alone with all that." He understood big feelings, whatever had happened. And while he hadn't the experience with them as some did, he understood they could be debilitating. Perhaps she had experienced something awful in her past. Her body was hot from her tears, and he soothed her as best he knew how.

"I'm afraid to ask, but do you want to talk about it?" He asked.

"Um, not right now," she replied once her tears had slowed. Standing there nestled against him with her head near his heart, he felt every bit as good as she had imagined. She could feel the steady beat of it against her chin. And he smelled good, earthy; the hint of whatever cologne he wore wafted around her.

"Can we try this again?" he asked gently as he stroked her hair.

Why hadn't she tried this first? Everything felt soft around the edges now.

She nodded.

"You'll let me know if you want to talk about something? Or break someone's nose?" he joked with a gentle smile. "I'm not a fighter, but I'll ruin someone's day if they ruined yours."

That got a chuckle from her, and she nodded through her drying tears. "It's nothing like that, but thank you." And she was thankful he'd come back. Maybe he was someone who would stay, after all.

Chapter 14

"That food should reheat well," she said quietly, still trembling. She had to change the subject, or she'd fall apart completely.

"Why don't you let me do that," he said. It was a statement, not a request. She let him familiarize himself with her kitchen while she composed herself.

"Why are you here?" she asked. "I mean, in Warren."

"I went to university here," he said, spooning his Pad See-Ew onto a plate. He licked the sauce from his finger. "Mmm, you were right—delicious."

"What is your degree in?"

He gave her that smile that crinkled the corners of his eyes. "World Science."

She surprised herself with a laugh. "That's not a real major."

"Right." His answering grin was boyish. Melanie realized that he was teasing her, and she didn't mind it one bit.

"I'm a retired real estate agent," he said. "World traveler. I do have a business and marketing degree, but a lot of my experience was in the field, as it were."

"You're like...forty," she replied.

"Forty-two," he said smoothly. "Forks?"

"In the drawer under the microwave." She cocked her head at him, "You're retired at forty-two."

He looked suddenly serious as he put their plates on the table, and his ruffled hair fell casually across his forehead. She wanted to reach over and set the strands straight. She wanted to crawl inside his head and know what he was thinking. This successful man had retired at forty-two and wandered into his grandparents' house in a nearly nowhere Kansas town. And why? Melanie relaxed back in her chair as the valium worked its magic and loosened her up. She felt intrigued and happy to focus on something other than herself..

"Yes. I'm trying to decide if that's a stupid decision or not. I'm trying to figure out if I should go back."

"Back to your real estate job?"

"Yes. And no." He waved his hand to indicate what, she didn't know. "I'm just trying to find my footing again, I guess."

"Oh," she replied, and took a bite of her Pad Kee Mao, more to stop herself from asking more questions than from hunger.

"What do you do besides the book thing?"

She smiled. The book thing. From someone else, it might've sounded condescending, but from Samuel, it sounded cute and sincere, like he was afraid of offending her by saying something else. "I don't know, I'm pretty normal," she said. "I like movies. Board games, video games."

"Indoor girl," he said, warm humor in his voice.

Melanie snorted. "You could say that. My life is my work, really. I eat, sleep, and breathe books."

Samuel smiled around his food. "Favorite movie?"

"It's a Wonderful Life."

"The Christmas movie?"

"No, the Italian one. *La Vita è bella*. Have you seen it?"

"I haven't."

She thought about snuggling up with him to watch movies in the alcove on the other side of the second floor and found she very much liked the idea. "Would you like to watch it sometime?"

"Are there subtitles? Like, it's in Italian?"

"Yes," she said, sure he wouldn't be interested now.

Samuel nodded approvingly. "Challenge accepted. I can't stand dubbed movies. They lose their meaning in translation. From what I've seen, anyway."

"Yes! That's what I think too!" Foreign films first, then maybe eventually they could play board games together. See how well they got along after a game of Monopoly.

They ate in relatively companionable silence for a minute.

"You went here?" He asked over his noodles.

"Library Science," she said shyly, feeling slightly self-conscious after talking about his career. She knew her path didn't make her any less successful than him, but it made her think about before, about going out, walking campus, taking classes. Now, she couldn't imagine it.

"You're a nerd," he said gently, with a wink.

She laughed, put at ease. "I certainly am."

The valium crept over her as they ate, giving everything a floaty feeling. This was what she didn't like about them, she remembered now, even for how chill she was starting to feel. They feathered the edges of the emotional spikes, released the roller-coaster-drop feeling she always got when the nerves got started.

When they both stood and took their plates to the sink, Melanie found herself toe-to-toe with Samuel, and she realized just how much man there was before her. Even with the meds, her brain started going a mile a minute, wondering what he would do, wondering what she would do, whether it would all be worth it.

Samuel saw the war in her eyes, the way her body tensed just seconds after relaxing. And he felt the pull between them, felt the chemistry, the whatever-it-was that attracted him to her and her to him.

He stepped back first. He wouldn't be the cause of more suffering for Melanie Montgomery. "Invite me back," he said, not dropping his gaze from hers.

He couldn't have known that giving her that space to breathe was just what she needed in the moment. The request didn't hang between them long before Melanie smiled, "I'd like that," she whispered.

"Even if that's tomorrow?"

"Especially if it's tomorrow," she replied, gratefulness welling up for all he had done.

He squeezed her hand and headed toward the stairs. Melanie followed him down to the door, her heart full of his kindness. She watched him walk down the sidewalk into the cooling night from her back stoop, and when she leaned further out the door to see him turn the corner, she didn't even feel the usual pang of fear when she got too far outside.

Chapter 15

B usy or not, he wanted to take her out. A proper date was in order. He wanted to watch what she did with those lovely fingers of hers at dinner. The love she had for the old books he brought in was obvious, and he'd been entranced watching her handle them. *Rare* books, he corrected himself. Melanie had explained that just because a book was old, that didn't make it rare. So far, he'd struck gold with everything he'd brought in. James Young's proposals had arrived via email without a fuss.

And he was considering having everything appraised at once. He'd initially understood the idea behind his grandfather's desire to farm the books out to different places, but perhaps he didn't understand how the world of rare books worked. Anyplace they took the books, they'd all get listed online, as he had learned from Melanie. Samuel was beginning to suspect that his grandfather was purposefully making the errands take longer because it amused him.

And it was never below his grandfather to get a laugh out of something like that.

But for tonight, he had paperwork to attend to at home. And he needed to decide where he was going to land. For now, at least.

Nana was sitting in her blue chair when he got back. She patted the arm of the chair beside her, beckoning him to sit. "Sit, Sammy, and tell me about your day."

"What are you sewing, Nana?"

She looked over her glasses at him. "You have never once asked me about my sewing, so don't aim to start now."

"You've got me there," he replied and went quiet, watching her move the needle and thread through the fabric within the hoop. The shape of whatever she was making wasn't clear yet, but he imagined if he sat there long enough, he would begin to see, to understand.

"They're tea towels," she explained quietly. "For the MCC sale in April. I get started on them early so it's a pleasurable task."

Samuel looked closer and realized the cloth she was working on did look a lot like the towels that hung over the oven door. "That's interesting."

She eyed him over her glasses again. "You're enthused, I can tell. You're a man, so I expect no less. I appreciate that you ask. I know that's genuine. Do you have a task you're taking your time at, so it's pleasurable?"

The words conjured Melanie's face so quickly and so clearly, he was almost knocked off the arm of the chair. The way her eyes smiled first, and the intelligence that swam in those grey depths...he was in awe of her knowledge of books, having had no first-hand knowledge of it himself. He'd taken bookstores for granted, thinking of them as nothing more than any other

71

business with inventory. He'd looked at Poor Oliver's as simply another interesting building. How wrong he'd been.

"I didn't expect to meet anyone while I was here."

Nana smiled slowly, the kind of knowing smile that the older generations have the privilege of using when youngsters discover the truths of the world. "I expect you didn't. Tell me about her."

"She's the owner of Poor Oliver's, the place I've been taking these books."

"I don't want to know about what she does. Tell me about her."

"She's..." What was she? Was she shy, or was it just a quietness? Though he felt like she might be the kind of person who wasn't actually quiet. She ran a bookstore, she must like people, surely she enjoyed talking to them, bantering with them when they came in. She was a far cry from the women in the big cities who had thrown themselves at him—and, to be honest, he'd thrown himself at them, too—women for whom money and gifts and the allure of status meant more than love.

"She's different," he finally said. "She's different from any girl I've ever met. She loves her work. I think she might love her work more than she loves to be away from it." He could appreciate and empathize with that feeling. He'd lived and breathed the real estate world for damn near twenty years now. He'd worked to work and then worked some more to get ahead of the pack.

"You know something about that," Nana replied, not looking up from her sewing.

"I didn't expect to find someone so much like me here in Warren."

Nana finally looked up, a smile on her face. "Careful there.

You sound like you've brought the big city mentality with you."

Samuel cringed. "I didn't realize I'd brought that back with me."

Nana patted his knee. "You'll shake it in time. You'll be chasing this girl, then?"

"I bet you gave the boys a run for their money when you were younger," Samuel joked. And it wasn't that he didn't want to answer Nana's question, but he was unsure of himself. He didn't have his footing here as he'd had back in Vancouver or Paris. It was like he'd lost himself somewhere along the way. Or he'd never had himself. He squashed the thoughts. There would be no going down those avenues right now.

Nana's smile was sly when she looked up at him, and her eyes sparkled as they must have when she was a third her age. "I did no such thing. They were the ones chasing me."

Samuel chuckled, still thinking of Melanie. She didn't seem one to chase boys either, whether it was when she was younger or now. For all her nervous uncertainty, he knew that wasn't who she truly was. He suspected that within her struggle was a smart, beautiful girl who loved so many things about the world. And he wanted to know her better.

Chapter 16

Nana was quiet for a moment before speaking again, choosing her words carefully. "I'm not sure about all those books," she said, turning the hoop over to tie off the thread.

"What do you mean?"

"Well, never you mind. We've gone to so many estate sales, I can't keep them all straight anymore."

He circled back to the thought he'd been having about how the books were getting farmed out. How, now that he'd been learning from Melanie how the process worked, it seemed odd. Perhaps his grandfather didn't understand how the trade worked, but that didn't sit well. His grandfather was far too smart for that. And as much time as he'd spent sussing out clients who were taking him for a ride versus those who were serious, well, this was starting to smell like a pile of something.

Samuel watched his grandmother sew for another few minutes, letting the rhythmic motion of the needle moving up and down soothe him and let him think. What reason could

Patrick have for placing the books in different places? Or was Samuel just overthinking the entire situation?

"I don't like that he's sending me all over half the state to different bookstores. That didn't come out right," Samuel corrected. What was he trying to say? "I've just learned a lot about the trade over the last few months. And it seems more prudent to simply take them all to Poor Oliver's and let them handle the final sales."

The needle moved up and down, never slowing. "Have you spoken to your grandfather about this?"

"I didn't think it wise."

His grandmother hummed at that, not answering him directly. "I don't remember the books he's been sending along with you," she finally said, the needle never slowing or pausing.

Samuel, hypnotized by the motions and how precise his grandmother's work was, almost missed what she said. "But where would he have gotten them from?"

Nana finally paused her work. She set the hoop aside and rubbed her eyes. "I am likely mistaken, son. My memory isn't what it used to be, and there are so many books up there, I doubt I'd even remember them at your age."

"Don't you have records of everything you've purchased? If they are so priceless, I have to imagine some of them have receipts."

"Not the ones from garage sales. He's had a few appraised over the years, but those have likely already been sold."

The sound of the garage door opening made them both pause, so Samuel wandered into the kitchen for a glass of water. Patrick came grumbling into the living room as Samuel was pondering the plant that Nana had had above her kitchen sink for as long as he could remember. Its long spiky leaves flowed from the hanging pot and sported bird's-nest-looking offshoots. He remembered being a young boy and thinking those tendrils would come alive at night and creep into his room. But as a young boy, it had been an exciting thought, to have a plant come alive like in *Little Shop of Horrors.*

Did Melanie have plants at Poor Oliver's? He couldn't remember seeing any, but he'd have to look the next time he was there. He wanted to bring her something besides books and coffee, and he could imagine a group of these, or something similar, having a lively time in the long front windows of the shop.

"You going to turn that water off? Seems we'll be splitting the water bill."

His grandfather stood in the doorway, his jacket over his arm.

Samuel snapped out of his thoughts and slid his glass under the stream again, then turned the faucet off. It wasn't like him to lose himself in memories like that, but neither was quitting his insanely lucrative job and going to live with his grandparents in Nowhere, Kansas.

"Sorry," he said, trying to sound sincere. He wasn't going to engage with his grandfather. It was never worth it. He'd spent enough of his teenage years getting earfuls of how he was supposed to be acting and how important those straight A's were.

"How'd the books go today?"

"Exceptionally," Samuel replied, giving Patrick his full attention. The man was as polished as always, and he'd probably just come from a drink at the 19th Hole with his golfing buddies. Samuel swept another look over the old man. No, this was more trip-to-the-old-office attire. That or the bank. It was an odd look for a man who was supposed to be actually retired, not just running from everything like Samuel was.

"And?"

Do not engage, man, Samuel reminded himself.

"Poor Oliver's didn't even need to list it. They said they should have a buyer interested and ready to purchase after the appraisal comes through this weekend."

Patrick looked like he was off somewhere else, then looked around the kitchen, his eyes lighting up when he saw Samuel. "How'd the books go today?" He asked again.

Samuel opened his mouth with a retort that asking again wouldn't change the status of his "sales," but Patrick looked so earnest that Samuel humored him.

"Exceptionally," he repeated. When his grandfather just nodded as though he was hearing the news for the first time, Samuel added, "They think they'll have a buyer without listing it."

"That's what I like to hear." All smiles at the second helping of good news, Patrick clapped his grandson on the back, and left the room, presumably to find his lounge pants and loafers.

Samuel took the atta boy with him downstairs to his basement apartment, the confusion about his grandfather's repeated question dissipating. The roomy basement was more than enough, but it wasn't inviting tonight. There wasn't much natural light down there, no smells of books and coffee to tickle the imagination. Melanie and Poor Oliver's was much more inviting, but he tried to tuck those thoughts away. He had loose ends to tie up between New York and Vancouver and Paris, and probably a few more in between. With a huge sigh, he booted up his laptop and opened his email. David had better be ready for a marathon session of filing with all the paperwork he was about to get through.

Tie up the loose ends, he reminded himself. Then think about Melanie.

Chapter 17

Her morning was spent pleasantly unboxing new books and merch while her time with Samuel played through her head. It wasn't just the giddiness of being near someone she liked. It was the compassion he had shown. Why would anyone do that for someone?

She tried to not think of it, to bury herself in the work she enjoyed. And it worked for a time. The new books looked so shiny and happy on the front tables, sitting among some happy flowers she'd had delivered from the flower shop a few streets over. The sunflowers felt as sunny as her heart did that day.

Anna Jane came waltzing with a bag that smelled like an early lunch and looked ready to pump her friend for information.

"You are going to tell me every last detail," Anna Jane said as she set the bag from Bistro Anis down on the sales counter.

"AJ, I had a panic attack and kicked him out," Melanie said smoothly as she tucked a wayward receipt back into the register.

Anna Jane was there in a moment with a sympathetic hand

on Melanie's arm. "Mel…"

"But he didn't leave."

"What?"

Melanie felt energized by the knowledge now. "I kicked him out, and he came right back. He's probably crazy, but I don't care. I like him."

"Detailssss," AJ prodded. "I need them!"

"Okay, okay. Let's go upstairs." Melanie grabbed the bag of food, and directed Jenny to man the register, thankful that her hourly employees were back. Then, she nearly sprinted upstairs with AJ in tow.

As they set out their meals, blackened balsamic chicken with strawberries and blueberries over spinach for Melanie and lentil soup with a crusty baguette chunk for AJ, Melanie described her night, embarrassing moments and all. She had to face it sometime, and she'd rather do it with her best friend than basically anyone else on the planet.

"Are you going to have sex with him?" Anna Jane asked casually as she nabbed a balsamic covered strawberry from Melanie's plate.

"Oh my God, AJ, he didn't even kiss me! I am the hottest mess of all time."

AJ's eyes sparkled with good humor. "The plot thickens. What will our heroine do?"

"Probably have a panic attack and pass out on the floor next time," Melanie said with a great sigh, then theatrically threw herself back into a faint in the chair. "Then he'll have no choice but to peel me from the ground and bring me back to my senses with a kiss."

AJ half-choked on her bite of baguette when she laughed, spraying crumbs all over the table, "Ha! I see. This is all part of your plan."

Melanie huffed and sat back up to stab at her chicken. "Yes, *Betrayed by My Body*, a suspenseful thriller in six-thousand parts. What will Anxious Girl do next?" She pointed at AJ with a forkful of chicken. "And may I point out that at no point did he so much as blink while I was crying and must've had snot on my face."

"Is he blind? Have you asked if he needs glasses?"

Melanie drifted back to the memory of him on the first day he'd come in. "He was wearing glasses the first day he came in. Tortoiseshell, so he looked impossibly nerdy. I never thought that could look so sexy on a man. He probably lost them doing something manly. Have you seen his arms?"

"He's not my type, but I can appreciate a person dedicated to the gym."

Melanie's response was an appreciative hum that had nothing to do with how good her balsamic chicken was.

"I'm still waiting on an answer from the prude across from me."

It was Melanie's turn to steal a wayward piece of crunchy baguette from AJ's plate. "I haven't decided. I think I'll let him kiss me first."

AJ started clearing their lunch mess. "Keeping your cards close, I see."

Melanie gave her a saucy grin and the pair headed back downstairs. The knot in Melanie's belly felt more like anticipation instead of something to fear. As the day wore on and she carefully cleaned sticker goo off covers and hummed through rearranging stacks in the cookbook section, she wondered what it would be like to kiss Samuel Reid. Would his beard tickle her face? Would it be a good kiss, or would he disappoint in that department? She had a feeling he wouldn't, and the anticipation grew. Perhaps she could invite him back in tomorrow and see for herself.

When the phone rang near close, Melanie cursed whomever was calling as she tried to shut down the store. She still had invoices to go over before she was officially done for the day, and she wanted to relax with a movie upstairs.

"Hello?" she asked tartly. Find out what they needed and breeze them off the phone, that was all she needed to do.

"I know, I know, it's too close to closing. That's why I'm calling though. I wanted to extend my congratulations on your sale, dear girl. Welcome to the club."

"Oh, Shannon!" Melanie wended her way through the shelves to grab a cup of coffee and wandered to an overstuffed chair. She'd never met him in person, but the owner of Jackson's, a large bookstore in New York, had kept a lively friendship with her by phone and email. They had met over the phone for the coordination of a sale of multiple books to be put into a collection. That had been an effort that she wasn't certain the buyer had fully appreciated. It had continued naturally as encouragement and enthusiasm for the other's success. Melanie loved the group of booksellers she had come to know and love during her time at Poor Oliver's. To have such a wonderful group of humans rooting for her success come hell or high water, well, that was something.

"I feel like it's not real yet," Melanie laughed.

"You won't for a while yet. Trust me. Everything going well at the store otherwise?"

The thought of "otherwise" made Melanie's stomach do a slow turn. The "otherwise" could be a good thing, she reckoned, especially if she looked at it that way. She was an adult woman. She could flirt, could kiss, could do whatever she wanted with whomever she wanted. Her issues didn't have to get in the way of that. Bolstered, she got off the phone with Shannon feeling calm and relaxed. A movie could wait. She'd get a few shelves rearranged, look over the invoices, and then maybe give Samuel Reid a call and invite him over for a drink.

Chapter 18

The bells on the front door jingled not long after. Damn, she'd forgotten to lock up in her excitement after chatting about the sale with Shannon.

"I'm sorry, we're already closed," she called without looking over at the door. She tried to shove a copy of *Frankenstein* into a shelf already crammed with various publisher's copies. If she could just fit one more...

"I know," a soft voice replied. "I'm here to fix that step."

Melanie looked down from her spot on the step ladder, the misfit copy of *Frankenstein* still in her hand. She hadn't thought he was serious about his offer to help. "Oh. Oh! Hello."

Samuel stood there in worn jeans and a white, short-sleeved button up. In the dying light, he was a hazy silhouette, his carved face softened by the sunset and streetlights. She was struck that she wanted to know what those lips tasted like, what it would feel like to run her hands over those muscled shoulders and through that wild hair. She could see the top of his glasses tucked into the front pocket of his shirt, and the image was so hot that she swore she felt him pressed against her from across the room.

God, she wanted him now. Just as he was.

She licked her lips to wet them and came down from the step ladder. Her whole body hummed to be pressed against his.

He was enraptured with each step she took toward him. Did she realize how impossibly graceful and lovely she looked, sauntering toward him in the dustmite-filled light of the setting sun? He yearned to know more about her, to hear her laugh, to watch her go about her business which she loved so much. It touched something within him that he hadn't known was there, a wanting to dedicate himself to someone else. He'd spent so many years on the run with work; how had he missed how amazing it felt to slow down and appreciate what was right in front of him?

Feeling emboldened by how warmly he watched her, she stepped up to him. She couldn't help the smile pulling at her lips. "Don't you have somewhere else to be?"

Samuel reached for her, sliding a hand over her hair. Melanie closed her eyes and enjoyed his gentle stroking, letting her cyclic thoughts fall away.

"I'm enjoying this view quite a lot." The miniature book earrings she wore bumped against his wrist playfully.

She couldn't help but smile, and a quiet laugh that pushed her breath over his hand sent shivers through him. "Surely you do have somewhere else to be than in a used bookstore after hours."

Melanie slid her hands up his arms, feeling the smoothness of his skin beneath her papercut fingers. She wanted so much in that one instant and it all flooded her throat at once. She merely kept quiet and waited for him to respond.

"No, there's nowhere else I'd rather be." His hands trailed through her hair to her shoulders where he dipped his fingers under the collar of her shirt. Melanie flushed with heat and held onto Samuel's arms, involuntarily grasping him tighter.

"Melanie?"

Her eyes snapped to his. The gold around his pupils was more pronounced in the dim light. In the moment before her eyes were guarded again, he saw her softness, that pliant vulnerability which all women possessed. What would it take to unearth the key to Melanie's vulnerable places?

"I'm here," she responded quietly, lost in searching with her eyes and her hands for answers to questions that hadn't formed in her mind yet. What did she really have to lose by getting closer to this man? He didn't push her to leave, no matter that he didn't *really* know what was going on there, but still. Screw all the others who treated her issues like something she could simply get over.

Besides, none of them possessed a first edition print of *The Woman in White*.

Taking a breath, Melanie leaned forward and pressed her mouth to his. Wholly present today, she could relish what she'd only been able to wonder about before. His lips were full and smooth, not what she expected in a man's kiss, and she nipped at them with her teeth instinctively. She felt him take in a sharp breath, and then he claimed her lips forcefully, wrapping his muscled arms around her like a weighted blanket, easing her tension even more.

She was kissing a handsome man, and she let herself be swept away on the feeling. It'd been so long since she'd kissed anyone. And it had never felt like this, like she was melting into a golden puddle. She was giddy on the feeling. But even as she relaxed, her belly rumbled. Energy she didn't know how to use vibrated through her. She knew the darkness was there, too, ready and waiting to swallow her whole. It warred with how good this felt, how amazing it was to have this man pressed against her.

When she set her hands on his chest, he pulled back immediately. "Are you okay?" His voice was husky, his eyes smoldering straight into her, into places only the endlessly repeating thoughts had known for so long. If he wasn't so hot, burning her from the inside out, she could have sworn he was cold water on a hot summer day, shocking her awake from the inside out.

"I'm..." Something welled up inside her. She strangled the tears. She would not cry in front of this man who wanted to stand in a bookstore with her. A handsome man with nothing better to do, but who didn't truly know her.

"My anxiety," she said lamely. How could she convey the compounded time of nearly losing the place she loved, of losing animals she could have saved if she had just been there before the fire started? Of thinking of those things, over and over and over, again and again, until the only place they stopped were within these walls? Here, they only badgered her when someone inadvertently triggered them.

His conversation with Nana, the moment he considered them similar, rushed over him again. His hand was in her hair again, soothing, petting, then lightly squeezing at her neck, releasing the tension there. "Is there anything I can—"

"Just be here with me," she interrupted, then chastised herself. "I'm sorry, I shouldn't have interrupted you."

"You don't have to keep apologizing. It's okay. Did I do

something?"

Melanie felt stupid. She was a professional woman, she managed everything from the relative security of Poor Oliver's. She'd gotten so used to her routine here, she didn't know what to do with these sudden deviations from her norm. Just knowing he might *suggest* they leave sent her into tremors half a dozen times a day. It threw everything off, tilted everything out of whack. She could order books and supplies, groceries, cat food online—and they appeared. All the normal things. She'd managed, she supposed, by not managing at all, by simply winding wool around herself until she was buffered from everything in the outside world.

And then Samuel Reid had gone and imploded everything.

She knew that wasn't true as soon as she thought it. This was about her needing to acknowledge her issues. But it was so much easier not to.

"No, this is definitely about me," Melanie said, cringing. "That sounds so awful, I—"

"My turn to interrupt." Samuel set a finger lightly on her lips. "You don't have to explain to me. I just want to make sure I'm not stepping on your toes."

"Not at all." Melanie snuggled into his strong arms. She felt comfortable here. "I feel like a kid," she confessed. "I haven't dated in so long; I think I've regressed." She laughed and looked up at Samuel.

"Are you...?" he left the question hanging. "That's an inappropriate question for a second date."

"I'm just busy," Melanie said simply, quietly, and nothing more.

"You don't have to explain yourself," Samuel said, again. "I want you, but not until the 'yes' I get from you is enthusiastic.

Chapter 18

And I made a deal. Show me the tools; I'm here to fix your step."

The grin that Melanie rewarded him with made him hold onto those words for dear life.

Chapter 19

He handily fixed the step—with much less whining than Paul would've done. Grateful, she invited him to sit with her at the rear of the store, next to a window that looked out on the cobbled street. The streetlights illuminated leaves that had blown in from the large trees lining the streets. She'd be sweeping them out of the store when the weather finally decided to turn. Now they were falling because it was late summer, and they were tired.

She'd been religiously taking her meds, and she was starting to feel better. The dry mouth she could live without, and her thoughts still cycled from time to time, but better was better. She'd even considered going to the therapist. Actually going there. Considered it.

And she wanted Samuel. And his company. Melanie smiled at the way he strolled over with his messenger bag slung over his shoulder, all casual male grace wrapped up in muscle and those worn jeans that seemed made for his body.

Samuel slid his messenger bag to the floor and sat with a

sigh. He might've lifted weights, but manual labor was another thing altogether. His shoulders and arms ached pleasantly, and he felt awash with what doing something physical did to a man. "What's something you want to do?"

"That's vague." She laughed. She enjoyed having this gorgeous man in her bookstore, asking her the kinds of questions she hadn't known she wanted to answer.

"Well, what's something you want to do for your books?"

For her books. She felt a smile pull at her lips. Warm eyes watched her, a quiet smile nearly hidden in his mussed beard.

"Is this the real estate agent learning his client?"

He chuckled, "Probably where I honed that skill, yes."

Then the words spilled out, coaxed by his gentle tone, which slowly sizzled a trail of heat down her back. "I want to go to the Antiquarian Book Fair in New York."

His quizzical look was charming. "There's a book fair for that?"

"There's art and old maps and photography and all kinds of ephemera. It's in the Armory on Park Avenue. It's huge." She felt a tug at her heart that she might never go—that she almost certainly *wouldn't* go.

"You've been before?"

Her insides were nibbled by anxiety somewhere deep and mostly out of reach. "I want to go," she said quietly. "I've heard so much about it, seen pictures and videos from the fair."

"New York is a magical place if you know where to look," he said.

She wanted to go, wanted to see the place where so many rare books and curiosities from her line of work came together. "Will you tell me about it?"

"Why don't we go sometime? I could fly us there."

"You fly?" she sputtered. "Of course you do."

Oddly, he felt like he shouldn't have mentioned it. His mother might've scolded him, told him he was bragging, but was he? Trying to impress this woman who had already left such an impression on him? "It came in handy if I was working multiple sales in one region."

The roller coaster feeling visited Melanie's stomach again. Leaving home *and* flying? She forced herself to smile. "New York is a long way from here. I'd have to get someone to watch the store first. Sometime, sure."

Sensing her unease (had he brought that up too quickly?), he changed the subject. "I brought another one." He didn't say that seeing her almost made him forget why he'd come there in the first place.

And he set on the table the single most valuable book she'd ever seen in person. If it was what it looked like it was, it would eclipse the potential of *Dorian Gray*.

She swore her heart stopped. Gone was any feeling other than shock. "Where did you get that? I mean, I know where *you* got it, but where did *he* get it?" Fear crept over her. Suppose he had dropped his bag and the book tumbled into a puddle, or he had bent a corner putting it into his bag, or...she stopped herself and took a deep breath. She let it out slowly. None of those things had happened. It was here safely now.

"Another estate sale, I'm guessing. And look," he said as he touched the clamshell box, Watching his fingers on the fine leather sent pleasurable shocks straight through her, and she had no trouble imagining how she would purr and arch into his hands just like a cat. Samuel spun the book toward her, opened it, then the cover of the book like he wasn't doing anything special, all the while Melanie felt the heat ratchet up, "Fitzgerald signed it for this woman on her twenty-first birthday. How cool is that? I've never seen history like this before."

Melanie was going to scream. She managed to gently take Samuel's hand as though she just wanted to hold it instead of getting potentially dirty fingers away from the most beautiful copy of *The Great Gatsby* she'd ever seen. She wanted to smell the book, but she didn't want to touch it. She wanted to stand out in the street with the book held high and scream about what had landed in her lap. And just as suddenly, she didn't want to be trusted with this sale, even though she knew at least three buyers who were looking for something like this.

"This is magnificent," she finally breathed, dizzy from either her meds or the prospect of another six-figure sale or both.

"Do you know what it's worth?"

She couldn't help herself. "It's the most valuable book that's come in here. I mean, it's nearly priceless."

Samuel didn't want to ask how much, but now he was curious. "I don't understand what that means in bookish."

"Personal inscriptions from the greats are rare," Melanie explained. "And if the appraiser can verify this copy's origin, we have a better chance of getting more out of the book. Plus, the clamshell. The box," she elaborated.

"But please," she continued. "Be careful with this book. I'd almost prefer you don't bring them here first. Go straight to the appraiser, then here. It gets me all anxious thinking you're carting something this valuable around everywhere."

"But I like seeing you all hot and bothered," he said with a wink that shot right through her.

"Oh. Well...hmm." Suddenly she very much wanted him to stroke her spine the way he had *The Great Gatsby*, for him to draw his hands seductively down her back. She took a deep breath. "Umm...I did want to ask about something. I'm personally interested in the first set you brought in. *The Woman in White*. It's always been....I mean..."

"You're saying you want the red books I brought in? I mean, not knowing its history, you can't sell it for as much anyway, right? You can just have them."

Melanie couldn't find her tongue. "I can't just...they're your grandfather's," she sputtered. "Ethically speaking...."

"Then I'll have it back. I can do what I want with it, right? I'm not contractually bound to selling it at this store."

She was on uneven ground. That he wanted to give her the set in the first place seemed so huge, so unlike anything she had known. It was surely only because he didn't understand the books' worth. But he'd been in real estate. He knew numbers.

"Let me think about it?"

"Of course. Leave them here for now. I know the books are safe here."

She was afraid of the silence, afraid she might kiss him again. "I have to get that big stack priced before tomorrow." She gestured at the pricing table.

He let her abandon the subject. For the moment. He figured they'd circle back around to it and how he could get his hands on her again before long. "How do you price them? Is there a database or something for that?"

"Oh, I price them on a whim. Throw some leaves into the wind and read them when they land." Melanie smiled at her joke. Teasing Samuel was starting to feel natural, easy.

He stared at her in silence.

"Oh!" And then he laughed. "You got me." He liked this relaxed, humorous Melanie. He hadn't expected that. Then he stood, stretched, and felt Melanie's eyes drag over him. The tension was delicious, and it made him want her all the more, but he could wait.

"I'll get out of your way, but before you do all that...." And he led her by the hand to the corner where sci-fi and horror met, a spot with only a view of shelves of books.

Her hands still clutched the book he'd brought while he kissed her.

Interesting, he thought as he nibbled on her bottom lip, pleased with the little moan it elicited from her. With her hands clutching the book, she was at the mercy of the very pleasurable work of discovering just how delicious those lips of hers were.

What he didn't expect was the way it affected him. How soft her lips were, how they parted at just the same time he began to part his. How his head spun with the scent of her, the feel of her in his arms.

If he had his way, he'd be spending as much time as he wanted discovering and rediscovering the soft secrets those lips held. He left wanting more of her than he'd had, and part of him wondered just how much would be enough, if such a thing even existed with the soft beauty that was Melanie Montgomery.

Chapter 20

He tinkered with the gas mower for an entire ten minutes before he knew it was a lost cause. Fixing things *inside* a house was more his speed. Nana would have to use the old-fashioned mower until he could get this beast to and from the shop.

Avoiding the paperwork that had been piling up in his inbox, he carefully slid the Fitzgerald book into his bag and set off for James Young's bookstore again. He'd have to start charging his grandfather mileage if he wasn't going to take the lot of books in all at once.

It was a bit of a drive to Second Day Books and walking in, he felt odd, almost as though he was cheating on Poor Oliver's. The off-kilter feeling didn't sit right with him, but he pushed on ahead.

"I have another book I'd like to have appraised," he said to the guy at the front counter when he walked in. It was a different person from his first trip here. He suspected this was the owner.

"Let's have a look at it." The guy held his hand out for the book, which Samuel suddenly felt reluctant to hand over.

When he finally did, the guy inspected around the outside of the book, flipped the cover open, fanned gently through the pages.

Excellent poker face, Samuel thought, then looked around while he waited. The building had no architectural interest like Poor Oliver's. In a strip center off a busy street, this place was the epitome of efficiency without an iota of charm. Identical shelves ran away from the front in rows marked with their genre. What Samuel supposed were the rare books were enclosed behind glass shelves behind the front counter. Most looked fittingly old, though he was surprised to see some books that looked modern to him. He'd have to ask Melanie how that worked.

"With the addition of the personal inscription, I'll have to verify this book more carefully than the others you brought in. If you could fill out this form, I'll call you once I have more information. I'll let you know ahead of time that this one won't be a quick process."

Samuel scanned the carbon copy paper. It was a standard contract between himself and the bookseller, standard terms, standard release. He filled out the form while keeping one eye trained on the guy examining the book.

"Do you have the receipt for the purchase of this book?"

"No. I'm selling on behalf of my grandfather, who found this at an estate sale. Like the others."

"Then he'll have a receipt of sale as well as the public information that's supplied for the estate sale. I'll need both of those items to move further on this other than simply telling you what the book is worth."

Samuel was at a loss. Melanie hadn't mentioned any of those things, and it felt like this guy was trying to make Samuel do all the legwork for him. From a business standpoint, he admired the tactic, but from his position, it was extra work that he hadn't planned on. The appraisal from the first set hadn't needed nearly so much. "I don't have either of those things with me, and I don't think my grandfather does either. As far as I know, these have been sitting in his attic for years."

The guy sighed and took off his glasses. "Look, I'm going to be honest with you. This book is worth a lot of money if it's what it looks like. The other one you brought me—the Oscar Wilde? It was pretty easy to verify because it was simply in excellent condition and checked all the boxes for its edition. This personalization makes this *Gatsby* special. Six figures special."

Even for the sales he'd made in real estate—hell, that 300-million-dollar deal in upper New York had been a *really* sweet deal, one he'd celebrated with too much champagne and too many cigars with David and the rest of the agents—his stomach did an odd jump at the number. Putting on his business hat, Samuel sized the guy up. He was being a cautious business owner, and that Melanie didn't take more precautions didn't sit well with him either. He imagined her taking business advice from him though and cringed inwardly. That wasn't his place. She knew what she was doing.

"I was the guy who brought the other set in, too. *Woman in White* or something. You didn't need all of that with that set."

"Ah, that was you. That was more straightforward. This is an item of much higher risk. As such, there are more steps we need to take to verify it."

He couldn't argue with that. "What do you need that will

help you the most?"

"I need something, anything, that can place your…grand-father, right? He's the one who bought it initially? I need something that can place him where he says he bought it. A book of this worth is going to get major scrutiny, and the more thorough a paper trail I can get on it, the better."

"Thank you, Mr…?"

"Just James, please. Jesus, man. I'm not that old. And I'm talking *any* kind of paper you have on this. I don't care if it's a handwritten receipt from 1897 or a journal entry from 1988 where your grandfather talks about going to an estate sale. Old newspaper clippings announcing public estate sales are fine. I'm not saying there's anything wrong with this book, but it's a big sale."

"I understand. I'm kind of the middleman here helping my grandfather out. Don't really know what I'm doing," he added.

"Some unsolicited advice, then?"

"Shovel it at me." Samuel fished his readers out of his front pocket and slid them on.

"Don't even try to sell this book unless you can 100% verify the path it's taken to get here today. I'm not talking from walking off the printer's press, just the hands it's moved through since—though if we can trace it that far, we're golden. Frankly, if it were me, I'd just hang onto it. Put it on display somewhere for guests to look at."

James clicked through a few things on his computer. "Here, look. Here's a similar book without a traceable history. It's languished on the sales website for over two years." He clicked a few more times. "And here's a past sale of another book in the same category with a verified history. It sold for more and within a week of its posting. Bidding took it higher than I'd expected."

"I get it," Samuel said as he took his glasses off. "I'll see what I can find."

"Do that," James replied. "I'll do some of my own digging in the meantime."

On the drive home, the same off-kilter feeling followed him. He needed to talk to Melanie about this after he spoke with his grandfather. There had to be a way to approach the subject with her without him seemingly questioning her professionalism or business practices.

Back home, he was met with the cold stone wall of his grandfather's denial.

"It's a simple matter," Samuel explained. "And you won't even have to do much. Around what year did you go to this estate sale?"

"It was the '80s, maybe even the '70s. No one cared. Find somewhere else to take the book. This guy's loss if he just wants to give you trouble."

"He's just doing his job."

"He's snooping."

Samuel doubted that, and he didn't like the defensive tone his grandfather took about it. Could his grandfather have his fingers in something he shouldn't? Just what, Samuel wasn't certain, but he was going to figure it out.

Chapter 21

U nsettled by the other bookstore and his grandfather, Samuel buried himself in paperwork and the hunt for information on the books he'd brought to Melanie.

Juliette had questions about the flat in Paris that he couldn't help her with now that they were months into ownership. He gave her the name and number of an inspector who could look further into the rat issue. If they've moved in after the initial inspection and sale, though, she was going to have an impossible time squeezing any money out of anyone. He delicately maneuvered around saying anything of the sort, though, and gently pressed her to contact the other inspector and an exterminator.

He spent an unsuccessful hour digging through his grandfather's old roll-top desk in search of an inkling of information on any of the books stored up in the attic. Being famously poor at keeping records was probably the only reason Patrick Reid had stayed on this side of jail. And he was so famously poor at it that Samuel began to wonder if it wasn't purposeful.

But they were just books.

He checked himself.

They weren't *just* books. They were the source of Melanie's revenue, her livelihood. And he saw how much they meant to her.

He slipped in the door of Poor Oliver's just after six and sought out Melanie. He wasn't sure how he'd broach the subject, but he'd figure it out.

"Oh, Samuel!" she said, delighted. "I'm glad you're here, I—"

"You're closed, right?"

He grabbed her hand and pulled her along toward the door. She hastily tossed the rag she'd been using to clean on the counter behind her. "Well, yes, but—"

"Do you have thirty minutes or an hour to spare before you need to get to pricing and all that?" He was so focused on how he was going to talk to her that he didn't hear the hesitation in her voice, feel the resistance in her form.

"Yes, I suppose, but…"

"Let's grab something from across the street. I have some questions about a book of my grandfather's."

He was rushing her out so quickly, she didn't feel like she could get a grip on the situation. "I don't go outside," Melanie said. The stoop felt foreign, like she was visiting it for the first time. The familiar vice tightened around her chest, squeezed her. God, if this was what women felt like in corsets, no wonder they did away with them. Panic squeezed her windpipe for good measure as she toed a half step closer to the curb.

You'll get hit by a car in the street, her thoughts whispered. *There will be a fire in the rare books when you leave, the cats will suffocate in the smoke. Oh, but they already did that, didn't they? And it was your fault. You left them alone.*

"It's right across the street." Samuel's voice somehow reached her, giving her something to concentrate on.

"Stop, please!" She dug her heels in and pulled back. "I don't leave," she said as she backed up into the doorway. Into safety. If she didn't leave, nothing else could happen. *Someone will break in while you're gone. They'll be hiding, waiting for you to lock the doors again.*

She saw him thinking, saw him trying to form words for what she was saying, saw him trying to choose what came out of his mouth. Good. It was better than Paul trying to haul her down the street and tough love her into "getting out more."

"What?"

"I don't want to go *outside*."

Something in her voice sounded like panic, and she looked almost like she'd broken out in a cold sweat. He forced himself to slow down, to give her time to think. He wasn't talking up a sale here, trying to maneuver someone into a purchase. He watched the panic and embarrassment rush across her face as time stretched between them.

"I don't think I understand," he said.

"I literally don't go out. I don't want to leave." Saying it, she felt almost powerful.

Samuel let his brain work before he opened his mouth again. Every time he'd asked Melanie to go out over the last weeks, she'd given the excuse that she was swamped with work or had an extra project to take care of, and he supposed he'd just started bringing take-out in all the time because it was guaranteed to get a 'yes' from Melanie. He hadn't seen her anywhere else in town, and he'd been so preoccupied with his own drama that he hadn't noticed. He *should* have been taking her out to the movies, to concerts, to Kansas City on the weekends, but he'd been wrapped up enough in his own paperwork pity party that he'd missed all the signs. There was a word for what she had, something he knew he'd heard before, but he couldn't put his finger on it.

"When's the last time you left?" he finally asked gently.

Melanie stood on the threshold and breathed in deeply. The air was sticky after the heat of the day, but at least it was cooling down. It smelled much different now than it did coming in through the windows. Here, outside the shop, the air smelled more like asphalt and late summer trees than musty pages and a blend of the town's attics, basements, and living rooms.

The hot tingle that had started in her calves when Samuel pulled her out the door ran up the back of her legs and over the top of her scalp. What if something happened to the store while she was gone? What if someone got in and the cats got out? They wouldn't survive on their own and her books wouldn't be safe. Someone might steal her private collection. They might vandalize the building, they might...but wait, the cats were gone. The cats were...*gone*.

"Melanie?"

"Mm?"

Samuel took her hand and squeezed her fingers. He stood a step below her so they were eye to eye. "So? When did you last leave?"

That was an answer full of shame. "A month," she lied.

Even that seemed to surprise Samuel. "You're telling me that it's been a month since you've stepped foot outside this building."

"I step outside nearly every day to bring the book carts

in." That was also a lie, and she knew that he knew it. She hadn't brought the book carts in in months now. Longer. She watched the realization creep over his face. And suddenly she felt two inches tall.

"Melanie, I mean it. Has it really been a month?"

She couldn't lie to him, but she didn't want to think about it, didn't want to confront the truth. "It's probably closer to six weeks. Eight. Twelve. Longer. I'm not sure," she mumbled. Why did it even matter? Groceries showed up on time, packages from the post office magically appeared on her front counter, and she had everything she needed there. It was like home. It *was* home.

Samuel touched her shoulders gently. Standing on the stoop eye to eye with him, she felt exposed, vulnerable. Why was it so hard to leave and be out in the world?

"Do you want me to bring coffee back?"

She waffled, terror coursing through her, telling her to run—flee back into the building—*right now*. If she didn't leave, nothing bad would happen. Part of her whispered that nothing *good* would happen, either.

"No. I want to do this." She hadn't restarted her meds for nothing. She hadn't done therapy over the phone for nothing. Right?

Still, the snake of anxiety twisted through her stomach and up her spine. That was where it lived. Everyone always talked about the stomach twisting up in knots, but that's not where it lived. It lived in her back, her shoulders, her hips. Sometimes her joints, her bones. And the pain of it was never far away.

But she could do this. It wasn't *that* long ago that she had gone outside, was it? A year ago, she could have gone out on the sidewalk anytime she wanted. And before that, she could have gone across the street to visit AJ at the Walnut Cafe. But… stores were a distant memory.

Melanie tried to bolster herself with a deep breath. "Yes, okay. Let's go. It'll be okay."

Her heart raced as they stepped away, but she tried not to look back at the questioning eyes of the windows behind her. It shouldn't feel like a betrayal, but it did. The possibilities of what could happen spun through her mind, warring with the valium.

When she looked up at the sky, it seemed to spin, like she was at the center of some great tornado. She looked up at the same sky out her windows all the time, even went up on the roof sometimes. This shouldn't be so different.

But it was. And the vastness of it—she'd forgotten how *big* the sky was. The blue of it careened up between the brick storefronts, and her eyes struggled to accept the clouds far off in the southwest. She'd watched sunsets and sunrises and storms from her roof before, though. All of it. She struggled to reconcile how this could be so different.

She wanted to laugh and cry and scream all at once. And Samuel stood there next to her, calm and relaxed like the world hadn't just turned on its head.

Overcome, she looked down at her feet instead, willing the dizziness to subside.

A laugh bubbled up within her and escaped her lips before she could stop it. Samuel stopped with her in the middle of the street.

"What is it?" he asked. "Are you alright?"

Melanie wiggled her feet. "The asphalt, can you feel that?"

Samuel looked down, too, at his caramel leather shoes and how they looked next to Melanie's cute green Chucks that hugged her ankles so adorably. The juxtaposition struck him, but his gut feeling was how good they looked together. What a strange thought. He'd never felt something like that before. "Feel what?"

"It's so…different," she said dumbly, entranced by the way the street felt.

Samuel was quiet while he waited for her to explain.

"I'm used to walking on smooth floors," she finally said, looking up at Samuel with an awe in her eyes that made his gut clench. He would never presume to call Melanie Montgomery innocent, but there she stood with the most innocent look of awe on her face.

He reached out and took her hand. And how could he not? He couldn't imagine what she was going through right now, but he could be there for her. "Do you like it?"

The laugh bubbled out of her again, and this time it reached her eyes as much as it reached some part of her deep inside that she'd kept locked away.

There they stood in the middle of the road. Samuel kept one eye out for any cars that might turn down the one-way street, but he suspected they wouldn't. At least not until Melanie was done with her quiet moment with the universe. Even if he didn't understand it all, he could tell it was important to her, and he was glad to be a witness to it.

Chapter 22

When they reached the Walnut Café, the evening crowd was thin, but Melanie recognized a few professors and faculty from the university sitting with stacks of papers and mugs full of coffee, working diligently. At the register, Anna Jane was working.

"Mel!" Speechless, Anna Jane looked from Melanie to Samuel and back again. Then, softly, "I'm glad to see you over here."

"Me too," Melanie replied quietly. The smells in the café were overwhelming. Espresso with an undertone of sugary sweetness. Savory foods with a vague undertone of griddle grease. The smell of hot fried potatoes struck her in her gut, then lodged in her throat. How could everyone just stand there smelling that and not want to gag?

"Can I get a decaf Americano tonight, AJ?" She managed to get out.

"Of course. And for you, Samuel?"

Melanie barely heard Samuel order as she took everything

in. Why should it be so different to be looking at a glass case of pastries and tables and chairs scattered around the neutral, cozy space than to be looking at books in *her* cozy space all day long?

But it was. It was so different.

And it hurt, Melanie realized. She'd been selling herself short by not leaving Poor Oliver's, and she hadn't even realized it. No, she had realized it, but that had been a long time ago, sometime before she stuffed her feelings away and forgot about anything beyond the bookstore.

By the time they had gotten their coffee and found a seat by a window, Melanie was hard-pressed to stop herself from running back across the street. She reached for a subject. "You seem to know AJ?"

Samuel shrugged, oblivious to the utter war raging between her mind and body. "I've been hanging around Poor Oliver's a lot, you know. And I reckon it's the best place to get coffee in Warren."

Melanie struggled to keep on topic. Was the store okay? She hadn't locked the front or the back door, and they were closed. Would there be a line of people there when she got back? Or *had* she locked the door? Suppose she'd accidentally locked someone in? What then?

She dragged her attention back to Samuel asking her how she knew AJ.

"Here, and we were undergrads together. We both ended up doing what we really wanted, I think. She's always liked this environment with lots of noisy people; I've always enjoyed an environment with lots of quieter people and an inventory that's usually even more interesting."

"If I didn't know any better, I'd say that books are more

interesting than humans to you."

Melanie felt a smile spread across her face as the statement tugged at her heart. "Oh, my mother would love to hear you say that. Some days that's true, but I wouldn't be in business, or have an interesting inventory without interesting people walking through the doors."

"Do you think that books should be kept under a glass case?"

"As opposed to, what, reading them? Handling them?"

"Sure."

"There's merit in that, sure. A text that's hundreds and hundreds of years old needs to be preserved. The oil on our hands, air, moisture, sun—they all destroy the pages slowly over time. Someday some of our books will be viewed in the same way. But only some, only the ones that deserve to and do survive."

Samuel smiled, "So, it's up to you to decide which books deserve to be preserved? That's a heavy burden to bear."

Melanie returned his smile, feeling something tug beneath her ribcage. "I'd read any book worth reading until the cover fell off. They're meant to be read."

Samuel slid a hand across the table to take Melanie's slim fingers in his own. Her hands were beautiful. And strong, he knew now. He'd watched her grip and heft huge boxes of books, run up and down the stairs with stacks of them, help customers in the doors with their boxes. He knew what strength ran just below the surface. And knowing that strength, he knew she'd take what he was going to say in stride. She was a business owner, and he was successful in his own business. They could talk about business particulars together. No big deal. Why it might stick a knot in his stomach, he wasn't sure.

Someone bumped their table and spilled Melanie's coffee.

"I'll go grab a napkin," Samuel said, grateful for another minute to find his words.

"It's not much," Melanie replied. Now alone at the table, she couldn't stand it any longer. Fear launched up from her gut and gripped her throat, like she'd actually eaten something fried and it gave her acid reflux. Her entire body vibrated with the intensity of it. She slid away from the table, trying to get a handle on what her body was feeling. But she couldn't do it. She just...*couldn't*.

Avoiding a questioning glance from AJ as she hurried toward the door, Melanie stopped short of grabbing the doorknob. That led back outside. Back out to where things happened. She shifted uneasily on the balls of her toes for a moment, whispering to herself. "Oh, God. Oh, God. Oh, God."

She squeezed her eyes shut and ran out the door. She peeked through cracked lids as she sprinted back to Poor Oliver's, holding her breath all the way across the street, trying to pretend that *Outside* didn't exist, that somehow the Walnut Cafe and Poor Oliver's were connected.

When Samuel turned around, the bell was jingling on the door and Melanie's spot at the table was vacant.

Confused, Samuel wiped up the spilled coffee and carried his drink and Melanie's up to the register, where AJ was wiping her hands on a towel and watching with interest.

"She must've gotten called away."

AJ's eyebrows disappeared into her bangs. "You should probably know better than that by now."

The tone in her voice carried a warning. "What, that was her anxiety? She just told me she didn't leave, but I didn't realize that it was...." And what was it? Could anxiety really do that

111

to a person?

"You don't know her at all." At AJ's icy tone, Samuel eyed the other side of the street.

"I'm trying to get to know her," Samuel replied, pushing back against AJ's ice with heat. "If her anxiety is that bad, shouldn't she be seeing someone about it?"

"Have you tried asking her that?"

"Of course not."

"Smart man."

Samuel felt his temper simmer. This was a woman defending her friend, though, so he kept a lid on it. "I like her."

"Then you'd better run after her."

Samuel headed across the street with coffee in hand, determined. Determined to do what, he didn't know. All he knew was that he needed to go be with her.

Chapter 23

When he didn't find her on the sales floor, he hesitated at the bottom of the stairs that led to her private quarters. There wasn't a human noise in the building, but he presumed she was here. Somewhere.

"Melanie?"

"I'm up here," came a mumble from upstairs.

She wasn't in the kitchen. It still amazed him how efficient and unique the space was. He paused to admire the circular windows with curtains that Samuel had a feeling Melanie or someone dear to her had made painstakingly, lovingly. The bookshelves that served as a wall between her living area and more book space. And he hadn't even seen all of it yet. He'd fancied himself burned out from the real estate business, totally disenfranchised and disenchanted with even the most unique dwellings. And then there was this place.

And Melanie. A strong emotion moved around inside him.

"Melanie?" He called out quietly.

"Here," came the faint voice—on his left, hidden within the

bookshelves.

Samuel wandered in, feeling vaguely as though he were disappearing into an enchanted forest, trespassing on some ancient creature's sacred ground. The shelves held many books that looked old and others that looked modern and out of place.

He found her sitting on the floor, wedged between two bookshelves, her knees hugged to her chest. This was her safe place, he knew instinctively, a place that held her without judgement. How could he make her see that she could come to him, too, and not run away from him every time she panicked?

She took a shaky breath. "I run a business—been running a business for years. I've managed fine. And then you came along." Her heated eyes snapped to him.

He knew better than to push, but he did anyway. "I rocked the boat, did I?"

The fire there smoldered. "You did. I didn't want to go across the street."

"Why did you?"

"You pushed me."

"Good."

They stared at each other, heat to heat. "Is there anything I can do to help you feel safer?" he asked.

Her heart bloomed at the question, cooling the heat. "Don't push me," she replied, feeling a smile pull at her lips even though she didn't want it to. How could this man push and pull at her in ways that made her do the things she'd resisted for so long?

"They say that life begins at the end of your comfort zone," he said, crossing his arms and leaning against the bookshelf.

"Did you have that on a poster in your real estate office?"

He laughed. "Right next to the one of a kitten hanging off a branch that said, 'Hang in there, it's almost Friday!'"

She laughed and the tension released. The feeling of wanting still pressed around them, but she had a need to show him her space, to show him that she could be in control. Going across the street had at once terrified and excited her. The feeling of the asphalt beneath her feet stuck with her, as had the slap of her shoes when she ran back. "Come." She stood and grabbed his hand. The warmth that went through her was calming, and Samuel squeezed her hand familiarly.

"A surprise?"

"Mmm, sort of." She led him through the shelves to the far end of the second floor where, one summer in a fit of boredom, she and Paul had split the cost of a screen and projector and attached it to the large, blank wall. Then they'd lugged up a few overstuffed chairs and a couch, and put down a soft rug in case they wanted to chill on the floor. She spent nights there occasionally—it felt like her own personal campground.

This hidden space between the bookcases could have been there for centuries, surrounded by books just as old. It reminded Samuel of his grandparents' attic, if only because it smelled like old paper. Scents from Melanie's apartment—spiced candle and dish soap—wafted through the shelves. His real estate brain admired what she had done here.

"This is a great place," he finally said, at a loss for words.

Melanie watched the man before her take in the room. He was all hers and all she wanted for now was this moment, this place of nonexistent time with him. She went to sit on the couch, and he joined her.

"And I like that you collect books," he said lamely, searching for words which seemed just outside his reach. Whatever was tumbling around inside him was bigger than the strangeness of his grandfather's books. It was bigger than anything he'd ever known. Samuel felt a sorrow for the things he'd missed in his push to be successful, in living the dream life that, if he was being honest, was more about his grandfather than himself. He hadn't built a business—or a *home*— around what he truly loved.

Melanie had those things despite her struggles. The things she loved best surrounded her all the time.

And what did he have?

He'd been so busy doing, he hadn't done any being.

Book collector. She wondered why she hadn't thought of that one before. "That's a new one. I like it. Do you collect anything?"

"Shoes," he said with a shy grin. He tried to conjure up other things he had loved as a kid. Had he had any fun? Surely that was in there somewhere, buried by time and the hyper-fixation on chasing success.

Ah, she had cracked the surface, and she wanted to know more. "Shoes? What kind? UGG slippers, preferably water-logged?"

He laughed until tears shone in the corners of his eyes. "I'll never live that down. I threw them in the trash on the way home, you know? They were ruined."

"You probably should've tossed them in there before that," Melanie teased.

Samuel wiped his eyes. "Point taken. And besides those, tennis shoes. Nikes and Converse. Chucks," he said, which earned a smile from Melanie. "I'll wear the hell out of these Ferragamos, but my heart's in it for the sneakers."

"Can I tell you something?" She picked at the fringe on the blanket.

116

"Of course."

"There was a fire." It was the Big Thing. Which was followed by lots of Small Things. But she knew now that the Big Thing had started it all. It might have seemed obvious to others, but she'd buried it so deeply it seemed to keep slipping her mind. Like the cats. She frowned.

"Here?" Samuel asked gently. He rubbed a hand over her shoulders and felt how tense they were. Unsure whether she wanted to be touched, he simply let his hand rest there.

The silence that followed wasn't uncomfortable. Samuel sensed she would speak again when she was ready. With Melanie's revelation, his view changed. Everything about the building was unique, Samuel thought, and she had obviously worked so hard to overcome the damage done. Both to the building and herself.

On the far wall, he thought he spied what was left of a fireplace mantle with ornate corbels, a testament to Melanie's eye for preserving history. This unique living area with its library-esque style and secret spaces—like this movie nook—were cultivated for Melanie's comfort...because *she didn't leave*. He didn't need to understand books to understand its appeal, but now he saw it cast in the light of her. Across the way, a flock of birds flew by one of the original oeil-de-boeuf windows. In the dimming light, they were magical, their presence a brief connection between two worlds: inside, and outside.

"We were finishing this upstairs area for me. Redoing the floors, strengthening the load bearing beams to support the weight of all the books that would be up here. It was a huge project." Those days came roaring back to her as she spoke, memories conjured from the great dark hole that lived within her. They rammed the fuzzy grey boundary of her meds and threatened to break through. But the barrier held for now.

"Someone had left some rags, canisters of finish, shut up in the bathroom. I'd been staying with AJ while the construction was going on."

Samuel had heard of these things and had thankfully never had to deal with them personally. "It started the fire."

"Yeah....yeah," she said, her voice quivering with the weight of remembering. "I'd heard of greasy rag buckets in restaurants catching on fire, but I had no idea this stuff could do that."

"Hmm."

"That fire was five years ago. And I thought I recovered, thought I'd moved on from it. Man, you should've seen me. I kicked ass at everything before that. At first, I thought it was normal, to be scared to leave because something would happen—you know? But then, I stopped going to my counselor, started having my groceries delivered, and...I...stopped going...anywhere, really."

"And now?"

What a question. Her stasis had felt so normal before Samuel. No, it wasn't just that. She thought she *was* normal. She didn't want to admit that she wasn't, though, that he'd opened up her world and made her want to go back out into the real world.

"Now it's different," she finally said. And Samuel was just being himself by asking, which apparently sometimes meant he'd push her. Even if she didn't like it, she had to concede that he was asking questions she really needed to start answering—not for him, but for herself.

"Will you come back?" she asked. If he said no, she could accept it, she told herself, even as her heart raced in anticipation.

Chapter 23

He laughed easily, and she felt the vibrations of *that* somewhere altogether different. "Of course. A challenge isn't going to keep me away."

It was an odd phrase, but Melanie couldn't stop the way her heart bloomed at the thought.

Chapter 24

A nd he did. Day after day, evening after evening. Days became weeks, and then it'd been a month. He liked the rhythm of Melanie's life. James Young had pushed the appraisal through somehow, and Samuel let Melanie think he didn't know that she was about to close on the biggest sale she'd ever made. And surely the copy of *The Great Gatsby* he'd given her wouldn't last long on her shelf either. She did a good job at hiding it, but every now and again, he'd catch her smiling lopsidedly while she was shelving books, and he knew it had to be about the sales she was making. That he was a part of that made him feel…wanted. Needed. Loved.

Wasn't that something?

But if she could keep her sales a secret to herself for now, he could, too. There was time for all of it. He'd taken to re-reading *Lord of the Rings* in the evenings, when he wasn't snuggling with Melanie on her couch watching movies and eating takeout. That was his new favorite way to unwind with a finger or two of whiskey.

All of her days were bustling, busy, moving as quickly sometimes as the days he'd left behind—rushing from meetings to showings to closings. He enjoyed helping with odd jobs around Poor Oliver's. He could see now where the new part of the building had been blended with the older side awaiting renovations. Melanie must've spent a lot of time and money getting everything back in order after the fire. And it seemed she had done it all by herself. What a burden to carry.

He was grateful that she'd let him into her livelihood, her safe space, and let him be part of what she wanted Poor Oliver's to become. Finally having something to *do* had released a pressure within him that he hadn't known existed. And when a lull came, it was almost always at the right time, allowing them moments between the shelves to kiss and touch. He'd let her set the pace, but maybe it was time for a little push.

She was fighting a losing battle, sweeping leaves from the foyer at closing the night he felt that rushing *need* for her. Something about the way she cursed the rustling leaves that kept blowing back in made him crave her. Something about how she looked in that skirt and tights and tucked-in teal shirt. Something about how she was *Melanie. He* knew no one else like her and that unsettled something within him that he could only fix by holding her in his arms.

After she locked the doors, he pulled her into a searing kiss. She dropped the broom and pressed herself against him as though she'd read his thoughts. He could feel the heat of her burning him from the inside out.

"I want you. All of you." She wasn't sure if she had said it, or if he had. All she knew was that she was ready to open herself to him.

Samuel felt spines and hardwood press into his back as

Melanie pushed him against a bookcase. Scents of old ink and paper and roses and lilies were intoxicating, dizzying. He had to remember not to lock his knees when she clenched his shirt, to breathe when she pressed her lips to his neck and drew them across his stubbled jaw.

In the haze of letting go, he felt the hands upon hands that had touched the spines. They pushed back—the leather, the paperboard, the protective plastic on the hardbound books. Dickens, Collins, Austen, the Brontës, and all the Victorians of rarer caliber—they all watched as Samuel pressed closer to the girl who cared so deeply about them.

To be a fly on the wall, no—to be a book on the shelf. A fly with the lifespan of mere weeks could never understand the history of a book, the myriad hands that touched, stroked, and admired such fragile life. The hands that touched other hands through the centuries, a connection deeper and more intimate than the million eyes of a fly.

Melanie's long fingers began to unbutton his rumpled shirt, and he melted into her spell. She was fae, some kind of fairy or sorceress that appeared from the mists to make him forget why he was there in the first place. Morgan le Fay, with her hair down all around him, weaving a spell of her choosing. The old legend rattled around inside him, brought up from ages ago when his mother had told him stories before bed.

Melanie stretched her arm back to flip the switch for the upper lights off for the store as Samuel's hands slid over her waist. They stroked down over the flare of her hips, his hands squeezing where her backside met her thighs. It sent that delicious liquid warmth straight to her core.

"I want you here."

Melanie's pulse quickened. "Here?"

Samuel hooked his fingers in the belt loops on her skirt and pulled her against him. "More specifically, I want you on the counter."

Had Samuel not had a good hold on her belt loops, she would have melted into a puddle of hormones. As it was, she felt the hot pulse of desire deep in her belly as she imagined Samuel pushing the books aside in the throes of passion. In the vision, he pressed her body into the pricing table, driving her higher in her ecstasy. The fantasy almost undid her. "We shouldn't," she panted, even as her body screamed for it.

Samuel's fingers worked their way under her shirt, teasing her bare skin. "And why shouldn't we? This is your place. You can do as you please."

He was right, really. She could have him anywhere she wanted. Grinning up at him, she lifted upon her tiptoes and drew him in for a kiss by the back of his neck. Their lips met slowly, teasingly, each taking slow sips of the other. She was having fun. Wasn't that what she was supposed to be doing? It wasn't like someone told her she couldn't, she just…well, it seemed so selfish to be enjoying herself so thoroughly.

Melanie felt her entire body trembling. With the books watching, the scent of them and him flooding her senses was hedonistic. She was surrounded by the past and the evolving present, and she wanted to surrender to it, to let herself go under for this man, for the books he'd brought into her life.

Samuel lifted her up and set her on the counter. She wrapped her legs around his waist, warm skin to warm skin, and pulled him close.

"I've wanted to do this since the first moment I saw you."

"No, you haven't," she laughed. And it was the easy laugh that got her, the easy laugh that would not have been so easy even weeks before. What had he done to her, this man who had burst into her world and opened her up, like the surprise of a good book, chosen from the shelf at random?

"You're not very good at listening," he breathed into her neck, finding the spot that made her moan, the spot that made lights dance behind her eyes.

And when he slid into her, she swore she heard the room, the shelves, the pages, sing like the leaves of many great cottonwoods. She let herself fall into the primal rhythm, moans of her own mingling with his. They fell together, meeting each other in a place of need as old as time itself.

He breathed her name as he thrust into her, and she leaned against the pile of books she needed to price for tomorrow. She hadn't known how he would feel inside her, but she hadn't imagined this. She hadn't imagined feeling as though something missing was now with her, against her, holding her so tightly like he would never let her go.

His warm hands held her up, held her up both body and heart, hands that did not judge her for what she was, but simply asked for her to do better, to give him more, more, more.

She sighed contentedly, relaxing completely in his grip. God, she felt good. Light as a feather. Light as the skim of dust that settled on the top edge of a book, ready to sail into the wind with a breath. Light as scritta paper.

And when she orgasmed, her world exploded into a million points of light and her eyes flew to the ceiling. In that haze of pleasure, her thoughts spiraled this way and that. *Samuel would know what to do with that old junky ceiling. The Samuel who somehow knew how to touch me just right. Who just made love to me on a counter of books.*

And just like that, her heart filled with the want of him,

and she pulled him against her in a crushing kiss, her elbow knocking a stack of books off the table. As they hit the floor, hardcovers thudding and paperbacks slapping, Samuel lifted his head in concern, but Melanie simply laughed and tugged him in for another kiss.

Her sweet laugh was enough to send him over the edge. He buried himself completely in her, calling her name as the scent of her and her books tumbled over him. He'd never had a release so very soul-pulling. He hardly knew where he was, but Melanie's hands in his hair brought him sailing back to that moment, to her.

"Where did you come from?" she asked, breathless, her vision full of him.

"Just down the street," he teased as he caught his breath.

She laughed more quietly this time, then nibbled at his shoulder. "Thank you," she whispered. "Thank you."

Chapter 25

When they finally tumbled upstairs and slept, she dreamed. Outside, in the depth of the summer, with the crickets singing, she danced with Samuel: a waltz under the light of the crescent moon and the constellations wheeling overhead. They were both barefoot, and she felt—for the first time since childhood—the grass beneath her feet.

"I don't know the steps," she said, breathless.

"Here," he said. "Stand closer to me. Your hands go like this." And he set her hand on his arm and clasped the other in his and drew her closer.

She could feel the heat of him then, smell his cologne. Her heart hammered in her chest when she looked up into his eyes. They shone silver in the moonlight, reflecting the stars back at her.

"What if I'm no good?"

"I'll lead—I won't lead you astray. Here..." He showed her the steps under the spinning sky as the moon watched and the dewy grass memorized their movements.

As he counted off the steps, she could feel his warm breath on her cheek. His eyes never left hers.

"There you go, you've got it," he whispered. And in the moonlight, she could see his smile.

All she felt was him. The way his hand felt in hers, his palm pressed to hers, the strength of his arm. And so they waltzed with stars in both their eyes until she awoke.

Still lost in the dream, she reached for him in the new morning light.

He rolled over and threaded a hand into her hair, a soft smile on his lips.

"Do you know how to dance?" she asked with a drowsy smile.

Samuel sent her a puzzled look that might've been sleepier than anything. "Dance?"

Her heart leapt as she thought about her dream, about the realness of it. She almost felt she could simply walk outside and experience it. "Yes, like waltzing."

His chuckle was sleepy and adorable. "I had to take square dancing through middle school. We learned the classic stuff, too. Why do you ask?"

She didn't answer him right away, just reached for him and settled her head on his shoulder. "You move like you know what you're doing. It's unbelievably sexy."

He smoothed her hair and ran his fingers down her arm to take her hand. Her palm tingled and the stars returned, and she returned to the dream, circling in his arms under the open sky.

She squinted in the bright morning light, both elated and

terrified of the dream's intensity and what it might mean. She couldn't think of the next year without Samuel. Hell, she couldn't think of the next day without him. Her life, her heart, were no longer her own. She shrank under the covers, pulling them up to her nose. How had that happened so quickly?

Where was he? She risked a peek around, but he was nowhere to be seen. Nowhere to be heard, either, when she held her breath and listened. Where was he?

Melanie took a deep breath, held it, then let it out. Wake Up and Worry had been her *MO* for so long now. Samuel was here somewhere. Maybe the bathroom. And she was here. Present. And safe. She slipped quietly from her bed and padded to the bookshelf where *The Woman in White* presently resided.

The beautiful volumes begged to be held, so she did, gently running her fingers along the spine of the first volume before she slid it from the shelf and snuck back to bed with it. Just holding it in her hands felt like a crime. But if she owned this set, she could hold it and read it anytime she wanted. Daydreaming that the books were hers, she carefully opened the cover and fell into her favorite story about the patience of a woman and the resolution of a man, beginning in that hot English summer many, many years ago.

Chapter 26

S amuel felt a jolt in his chest when he rounded the corner
and saw Melanie snuggled in her white blankets reading
a book. But surely any man would have that reaction to
the gorgeous woman who'd spent the better part of the night
making love to him. He could feel her skin now even six feet
away, every glorious, silken inch of it. It made him want to
drop his coffee and touch her all over again.

And God, that smile. That she didn't care about where he'd
been and what he'd done, that she didn't care that he had no
clue what he was doing with his life—that struck him. She saw
him as he was in each moment and didn't dwell on what he
wasn't.

"I was gone ten minutes for coffee, and I see I'm not invited
back to bed," he joked to cover the quiver in his chest.

Melanie's eyes snapped to his over the top of the book. She
looked almost guilty.

Samuel stood there in his jeans, wrinkled shirt, and bare feet,
steaming cups of coffee in his hands. With the machine set to

auto-brew every morning, the smell must've woken him up. It touched her that he had crawled out of bed to get cups for both of them.

"Oh my God, you're a saint," she said, gently setting the book next to the bed. "Uuugh, I need my meds."

She was reaching for the cup when he turned, unintentionally pulling it out of her reach.

"Can I grab them for you?" he asked. She looked so adorable wrapped up in the blankets with that pout on her face. He wanted to crawl back under them with her.

Melanie was too sleepy to feel anxious about the question. She just wanted Samuel to hurry back into bed with her. "Ahhhh, yeah, I guess. Bathroom, second shelf behind the mirror. The Viibryd. I can get it, though."

"I'll grab it," he said.

"Need. Coffee. Now," she said, swiping for the cup again.

The grin he gave her was positively evil. "It's still too hot. You'll burn your tongue."

She smashed her face into the pillow. She felt so at ease with him, she realized. When she came up for air, she grinned at him. "Okay, mother. Coffee now. Talkie later." He handed her the life-saving liquid and went to get her meds.

Once in the bathroom, he realized his mistake. In his eagerness to help, he'd assumed the task would be easy. But he was faced with nearly a dozen bottles. He read the names while searching for the one she needed *Xanax, Klonopin, Paxil, Bupropion, Rexulti.*

Her voice floated in from far away, and he unintentionally jerked as he pulled the medicine out of the cabinet. Other bottles toppled into the sink and Samuel's ears burned. He felt like he was snooping even though she'd let him in.

She appeared behind him, a robe over her leggings and tank now. "Did you find it? I'm sorry, I should've gotten it."

"Ah," he started, at a loss. "There's a lot here. I..."

Melanie blanched. *Way to go, Reid.* Open mouth, insert foot.

She reached around him and plucked up the bottles in the sink. "Yes, I'm a regular walking pharmacy. Welcome to my freak show."

"Melanie, I didn't mean—"

"I know," she said, her eyes guarded. She shovelled the bottles back into the cabinet and slammed the door, making the mirror rattle. "I just...don't let people in like this. I'm trying to lean into the hard feelings, but it's...*hard*."

"What does that mean?"

"I have to get comfortable with feeling uncomfortable."

"Would you like to try coming to my grandparents' home for dinner? They'd love to meet you. And there's an attic full of books for you to dig through." Samuel reached for anything that might help her out of the spiral he could feel coming, but even as he said it, he knew he shouldn't have. Why couldn't he get his footing here?

"No. I mean..." she cringed. "It was really hard for me to even go across the street. I just...there's so much the bookstore needs right now. It's a lot of decisions, too, and I don't know if I want a relationship on top of that." But she did. She wanted a relationship—with Samuel—badly. And she wanted to leave, she knew that now. She wanted to go out and about when she wanted, and she wanted to stay put when she wanted, too. But she couldn't stop the words from falling out of her mouth. If anxiety was good at anything, it was at pushing away anything she wanted beyond these walls.

The little pang Samuel felt at the 'R' word told him that he, too, had some work to do. "Then let me help."

"Help. Help with what?" She bristled.

"I worked in real estate; I know what works. I'll bankroll whatever project you want to get going, get you whatever you need. Pull that drop ceiling out, get new shelves, put a fresh coat of paint on everything, refinish the wood floors, whatever."

Melanie stared at him, dumbfounded for a moment. That he mentioned the very things she wanted to work on rankled her. That it must be so abundantly clear to whomever walked in that she needed to spruce the place up also wasn't lost on her. "That's...well, that's...why? I don't need your help. Are you saying I need a man here to help me out?"

Samuel recoiled as though he'd been shot. "Oh, God, no. No! I just mean—"

"I can wield a bottle of Drano by myself, thank you."

Samuel felt himself smiling despite a warning somewhere deep within his heart that this was more dire than he thought. But yes, he thought, the other half of his heart cheering at the idea. He'd been stuck making money for what? To live a bachelor for the rest of his life and die with it all in the bank? And here was a woman he thought he was growing to love. What better place to use his money? He didn't notice the war waging on Melanie's face or her clenched hands. "I'm certain you can. And I'm not saying you need my help, but I'm here and I *can* help."

It didn't matter that he was offering to make her dreams come true. It felt like he was pushing the changes at her, like it wasn't her decision to make. "I feel like a child. I feel like you're taking care of a child. You're too nice. Offering to help me fix up the store like it's...like it's some kind of charity project."

132

"You're a grown ass woman. You know you're anything but that."

God, he was right, but she couldn't bring herself to say it. "I just think all the time about how much time I've wasted on this, and now you're wasting your time on me."

"Melanie," Samuel growled.

"You're not going to change my mind about this." She turned to go but was blocked by Samuel's body. She had the urge to poke him in that chiseled stomach of his but thought better of it. She'd probably only hurt herself in the process. The sinking feeling outweighed the good feelings of their sleepless night.

Samuel held his hands up and let her go around him, but he followed her into the kitchen. Good. They both had breathing room out here. "I'm going to quit arguing with you. Let me just say this: you are welcome at my grandparents' place anytime. In fact, I want you to come there and meet them. Quite a lot. I like you. A lot. But I don't know what else to do or be for you. I don't know how to move forward."

Melanie's laugh was bitter. "You don't have to *do* or *be* anything for me except yourself. Keep being kind to me. Quit overthinking things. I have my stuff to figure out and you have yours. This is who I am. Take it or leave it."

She interrupted him when he opened his mouth to reply, "Just...I have to find my own way, Samuel. I want you. I want you so badly, but I'm not going to push myself more than I can handle. You've been really good about pushing me just the right amount, but this is too much too fast. I need to slow down."

"I want you to find your way." Samuel's voice was raw with emotion. "And I want to be with you too. I don't want to stand in the way of your progress. I'm sorry if I pushed too hard. I don't want to do that again."

He reached for his bag and saw Melanie's eyes follow the trajectory. She wanted to ask if they were breaking up, but there was nothing for them to break up—they'd never made this official. "Well, I guess that's that," she said.

Samuel had the nerve to look confused, a look that was out of place on his perfect face. Except for that beard, which she wanted to run her fingers through even now, to feel it tease down her neck with his lips. "You misunderstand me," he said.

"I understand you perfectly," Melanie said, chin up. "And I get it. I need to figure my life out. So, I will. Have a good day, Samuel."

"Melanie," his voice was softer now, but she wasn't going to let him push her anymore.

"I'll call you," she said, and words sounded hollow even to her. They were meant to hurt and hurt they did.

He squeezed his eyes shut, then looked back at the beautiful, hurting woman across from him. He saw the need in her eyes, but he wasn't going to make her do anything. She had to choose herself, choose to do things for herself, not for him. It hurt, and all he wanted to do was reach across the space between them, but instead, he picked up his bag, went down the stairs, and let himself out the back door into the gloomy morning. The air was as heavy as his heart felt.

Chapter 27

Melanie jumped off the scale with a sinking feeling in her stomach and stalked back to her office. Down eight pounds. And she'd not had that to lose to begin with. Maybe if she laid off the Viibryd for a few weeks and really concentrated on getting her calories in she should...

But why take it at all if Samuel wasn't going to come around? And she did *want* him around if he was going to push her like Paul did. Sure, a nudge here and there was fine, but he'd crossed a line that she wasn't willing to negotiate.

She shut the book whose pages she'd been trying to count. She was too upset to handle rare books today, and she was liable to tear a page. She wasn't focused. And it was all Samuel Reid's fault.

He'd slept with her and given her the most mind-blowing sex of her life, then offered to bankroll her dreams, and what had she done? Kicked him squarely in the balls and anxiously talked him right out the door. Again. Not that he'd helped himself there, though.

She had a bad taste in her mouth, and she knew what it was. Pride. *Swallow or spit*, she thought wryly. But she couldn't just yet. She needed to get to this in her own way, on her own time, and Samuel Reid wasn't going to bully her into it.

Jenny poked her head into Melanie's office. "Is Samuel coming by today? We could use some help moving that weird shelf in the kid's corner."

The sinking feeling dropped lower. "No, he's not."

And probably won't ever again, she thought.

"Okay, well. Maybe Paul can help. Oh! And there's a message for you from H. Delbrook. Something about the book he bought from you," Jenny said in a rush. "I'm sorry, he was really vague, and I couldn't get anything else out of him. He only wanted to talk to you."

Strange. Perhaps he wanted to thank her for the book or had a question about the Fitzgerald she'd given him first dibs on. He'd bought several of the very rare books which had come in over the years, but she'd never known him to be vague or off. She grabbed the phone and dialed his number.

The pleasantries were short.

"I had a call from a James Young who says he owns a bookstore near you," Hans said, the German accent thick today.

She hadn't heard that name spoken aloud in awhile, despite seeing it often on appraisal paperwork. Despite being another member of the ABAA who should've had her back, he had made it clear that after the fire, he'd hoped she didn't reopen. So whatever he was sticking his fingers in couldn't be good news. "Yeah, he runs one about two hours from me. He did the appraisal on your book. And the Fitzgerald you want."

"Hmm, yes, well," Hans said, mumbling something to himself

that Melanie couldn't understand.

"I'm sorry, what was that? I can't quite hear you," she said.

"This book was stolen."

Suddenly dizzy, Melanie sank down into her chair. Then, just as quickly, she was back on her feet and pacing. This was her worst nightmare. Even after all the precautions they took mailing these books, there was still a chance for theft. She calmed herself. All was not lost. She wasn't sure how James would've gotten involved in this, though. "From the mail? We can absolutely open a case for it. I'll make sure to have my bill of sale ready. The package was insured, as we agreed, and you were supposed to be the only one authorized to sign for it."

"No, no, my dear. I mean you've sold me a book that was stolen from a rare collection a number of years ago."

Her heart beat unevenly and the ground tilted under her feet. The sound of her heart thrumming in her ears wasn't a side effect of the meds this time; she recognized real panic when she felt it. Then, she thought of Samuel and where he'd gotten the book and felt better. Estate sales, especially from the no-so-distant-past were notorious for the lack of a bill of sale. The book wasn't a fake or a forgery; she'd been certain to examine it. She found her words. "I can assure you that isn't the case. I know the person who brought the book in personally. That edition was purchased from an estate sale; the family would have gotten it a number of years ago, but I can assure you the origin is legitimate. Besides, James Young appraised it. If he's calling you now…"

Hans hummed around that while Melanie paced through the shelves.

When his silence continued, she blurted out, "I'll look into it again. There's just no way this book was stolen." She took a deep breath and held it for a few seconds, then let it out slowly. This wasn't going to go anywhere if she broke down on the phone with a client. Another deep breath, hold, and slowly let it out. There, that was better.

"If there are two copies from the same print run in such excellent condition out in the world, it would also lower the value. Whatever the case, this needs to be looked into." Hans sounded irritated, but professional.

"Absolutely it does," Melanie soothed, as much for herself as for him. "Will you email me what you learned?" She knew better than to question the man's judgment. He'd been in the business longer than she'd been. Longer than she'd been alive, probably. She'd get a paper trail going, make some phone calls, sort this all out. And James Young might have been in the business longer than she, but that didn't mean he could suddenly start mucking up her sales without speaking to her first. It might have been unofficial, but they were booksellers. They had a code.

She wouldn't tell Samuel, yet. This was obviously just the product of James Young the Sexist Jerk trying to stir up trouble where there was none. Or perhaps there *were* two outstanding copies from the same print run. And if Hans thought that lowered the value, well, they would have to see about that. If she could get someone else involved in bidding, they would certainly see about that.

Chapter 28

"What's that you've got there?"

Samuel looked at his grandfather over the top of his reading glasses. He was in no mood for his grandfather's needling today. He was worried about Melanie, and each mistake he made as he worked darkened his mood even further. If he'd been in his office in Vancouver, Kastie or Meghan could have whipped all this information into a spreadsheet in ten minutes, and mistake-free at that. He'd been sitting there the better part of two hours trying to make sure the formulas for each column were correct. Being uncertain was driving him crazy.

"Quarterly taxes. I've got to get the payments for these books in order. What have you done with all the receipts from the bookstores?" He could have sworn he'd left them sitting on his desk in the basement guest room.

"That's nothing you need to worry about," his grandfather said, his tone clipped.

Samuel looked up at him sharply, ready to meet his grandfather blow for blow. "I have to report this income," he said. "It's not insignificant."

"I said don't worry about it. If you were smart, you'd take the cash and keep it to yourself."

Samuel opened his mouth to snipe about getting audited but stopped himself. His grandfather wouldn't care. "Where did you get the *Dorian Grey* I took in? Or the *Woman in White* volumes...that red set?"

"Estate sales, son, like we talked about. A few others from auction, and enough from garage sales to make up for the time I spent searching through swill."

Samuel saved his spreadsheet and turned his full attention to his grandfather. "So what you're telling me is that you don't have original sale receipts." He knew the answer to the question already, but he wanted to push it again, to see if the old man stuck to his story.

"I don't know why that would be pertinent anyway."

"Some places require those for the sale."

"Then don't sell to those places. Someone out there wants it bad enough."

Samuel ran his hands through his hair, then over his face. He'd had his reservations about this venture, but stupid him, he'd chosen to go ahead instead of learning how to relax after fifteen years of running and pulling seventy and eighty-hour weeks. "Fine. Fine. Just let me get this done."

His phone rang and, instead of ignoring the local number, he took the call. Anything to get his grandfather to leave the room. Thankfully, he did.

"This is Samuel." He saved the spreadsheet again, more out of paranoia that he hadn't saved the time before and might lose what little he'd gotten done. He wondered if Melanie knew how to work these better than he did. He'd have to ask her for some pointers.

"Samuel, James Young at Second Day Books."

Samuel idly clicked into a game of solitaire. "What can I do for you, man?"

"I have a bad feeling about...well, I have some news about the copy of *Gatsby* you brought in."

He abandoned his game and reached for a notepad and pen. "You found something on it? But you appraised it and it sold. I thought that was that."

James cleared his throat, "Well, yes and no. Not yet. It's a book that's been...at some point it was stolen. The Fitzgerald. And maybe the Wilde, too." He added quickly, "I'm not saying your grandfather stole them or anything. Just that one or both may have been stolen at some point in the past."

Samuel set his pen down. The dark mood grew, and he felt the beginnings of a real headache. "Obviously I don't want that. So, what *do* you know?"

"There was a collection in Minnesota with a copy of that Fitzgerald with the same inscription. It's almost identical, but I'm having them send me over what they have on it. They're mailing it, of all things, so it'll be a few days before we know more. It could be another copy of the book, though. Not yours. It would just be a very strange coincidence."

Samuel kicked back in his chair and hung his head off the back. "Well, let me know what you find out. I can tell you I have no desire to be a part of this. And Poor Oliver's—"

James's tone changed. "What's Poor Oliver's got to do with this?"

Samuel sat up quickly, no stranger to noticing changes in the nature of a deal. If he wasn't mistaken, this was the *greed* tone he'd heard before in many a client. Was Poor Oliver's competition for this place? He decided to tread carefully, whatever the reason. Best not to tell the man the book had already sold. "I'd considered taking that and other books to Poor Oliver's as well. Should I not?"

Samuel could almost hear the gears in the guy's brain turning. "I wouldn't bring rare books anywhere but Second Day Books if I were you, but it's a free country."

"Poor Oliver's not reputable or something? And I thought you weren't supposed to appraise and sell at the same place. Ethical conflict or something." Samuel grabbed his pen again and wrote *James Young competition* at the top of the notepad.

"They're just new in the rare books game. Comparatively speaking. I've got at least two decades of experience on her. You could submit for appraisals there instead, then bring your books to me. I can guarantee I'd get you more for them."

Ah, 'on her.' So, it was personal with this guy. Samuel got a jolt of jealousy as strong as the whiskey he now wanted with his imagination wondering just *how* personal Melanie's relationship with this guy was or had been. They were both booksellers—had probably known each other for years. Samuel felt a strong desire to simply hang up on James, but he knew from experience that that didn't make people go away. He quashed his jealousy down as best he could. He would definitely ask Melanie about this guy. She was the one who recommended him. "Well, thanks for the head's up. Oh, do you happen to know the town where this book supposedly came from?" So long as it wasn't Silver Creek, Minnesota. Please not Silver Creek.

"Yeah, I've got it here somewhere. Hang on a sec." Samuel heard shuffling papers in the background. "Silver Creek. Silver

Creek, Minnesota. Must be a real small place."

For the love of God, Patrick, Samuel thought. "Thanks, man. I'm going to keep checking into stuff on my end. Keep in touch."

He set the phone down with a groan. It had to be the same book. So, either Patrick had a stolen book, or Patrick had stolen the book. The more he thought about it, the more convinced he became that this was all very not good. He would've been too young to remember his grandparents moving from Silver Creek, but he bet his parents did.

His stomach clenched and twisted. He'd gone into this an unwitting accomplice. Guilt that could not find a place to land tore through him. Anger at his grandfather wasn't far behind, hitting him like whiplash.

And he needed help, damn him. He pulled out his phone and texted his parents, checking his watch as he did. They'd be watching Wheel of Fortune and eating their dinner. It was pork chop and pierogi night.

Bolstered by the thought that his parents would have answers, he headed out of the house on an errand. He decided that Melanie had stewed long enough. There was something he wanted to get for her, and he hoped that it would breach the gap between them. Because he, for one, hadn't had nearly enough of her dark, tousled hair and the heat of her skin against his. One night was not going to be enough for Samuel Reid, and he had a suspicion that Melanie Montgomery felt the same way.

Chapter 29

He was contemplating a second workout when he got a text from Melanie. Just seeing her name on his phone sent a rush of relief through him. *I'll take you up on dinner at your g-parents' house.*

The relief that she'd contacted him was an unfamiliar but not unwelcome feeling. He'd been worried about her. He knew, though, with the certainty of all things instinctual, that he shouldn't push his attentions on her or smother her with questions if she was feeling anxious. Giving a person room to breathe was something he supposed he'd always wanted in a partner, but he'd never exactly been given the chance to show that from his end.

But he was surprised that she was the first one to make contact after their...was it even fair to call it a fight? Samuel asked Nana if they could have someone over for dinner and ignored the raised eyebrows from both grandparents. Knowing Melanie might need time to adjust to the when of it, he angled for the next night. Maybe if she had 24 hours to prepare, it would help her out.

Yes, what about tomorrow night?

Will you walk with me there? Then, *I'm sorry.*

He couldn't say no.

He'd found what he thought was the perfect gift, and now that she was coming to him, perhaps it would be a nice distraction when she got to his grandparents' house. He really did want her to have a good time.

And damn it, he wanted to see her. He missed her something fierce, and he missed the bookstore. It felt worldly and homey, two descriptors which shouldn't have worked so well together, but somehow they did.

At around ten 'til five, he trekked down to Poor Oliver's to meet her. The walk left him grateful for his white short sleeve button up, but it wasn't as bad as downtown Vancouver in the summer. No matter how clean the city, there was always that memorable *city* smell, kicked into high gear with the heat. Here, it smelled like…air. Probably the way it was supposed to.

On the way, he turned the book situation this way and that in his head. The anger and odd guilt he'd felt back home had dissipated. This would get figured out swiftly and be a thing of the past in no time. Like many snafus in the real estate world, there were things going on behind the scenes that clients were better off not knowing. He and James Young could figure this out between themselves.

His parents' responses had been lackluster. Patrick and Nana had left Silver Creek in '81 and there seemed nothing untoward about their leaving. They had wanted to downsize and at the time, Nana's mother was still living in Warren but needed assistance. So, to Warren they went. The home that was once

Samuel's great-grandmother's became his grandparents' home, great-Nana eventually passed, and someday, the house would go to him.

The thought, which he used to keep far from his mind, now seemed somehow more and less real at the same time. With its walls tangibly around him, the intangibility of its ownership eluded him. He couldn't comprehend owning a classic Victorian home in Warren, Kansas. Lofty penthouse in Paris? A condo in Vancouver? A timber frame mansion in the woods of northern New York? Sure. But a Victorian confection in Nowhere, Kansas? It escaped all sense and reason.

When he met her at the back door of Poor Oliver's, she was all wide eyes and bouncing feet in a summery blue and white striped dress. The effect was stunning.

"You're beautiful," he said quietly as he stepped onto the sidewalk.

Her eyes crinkled briefly in a smile that shone through the worry in her eyes. "You think so?" She tugged at her dress. "I wasn't sure what to wear and I haven't really been outside, so I'll probably burn easily, and—"

He silenced her by sliding his arms around her and pulling her in to kiss her forehead gently, then her nose. Finally, he saw the nervousness leave her eyes. She giggled.

"*You* are beautiful, and I'm going to kiss you now," he said, voice low.

Her smile remained, but it turned shy. "Okay," she said, caught up in the heat in Samuel's eyes. Even after she'd tossed him out—for the second time—he still looked at her like he enjoyed her company.

Samuel closed the distance between their lips, then was

146

pleasantly surprised when Melanie took charge of the kiss, fisting her hands in his shirt as though she wanted him closer.

Happy to oblige, Samuel slid his hands down her back as he kissed her until even he was dizzy. Whatever lotion or moisturizer she used, combined with the warmth of her underneath that scent, was intoxicating. He nibbled at her bottom lip and reveled in the contented sigh she gave him in return. Wanting to go deeper, but knowing they had somewhere to be, he pulled back reluctantly. His hands still resting on her neck, thumbs tracing the line of her jaw from chin to ear, he realized how glad he was that she'd decided to do this.

"I'm sorry for falling apart. I'm sorry I threw you out. I'm sorry for, well, everything," Melanie said in a rush.

"There's nothing to apologize for," Samuel replied quite seriously.

"Of course there is. I'm being a jerk. I keep pushing you away like I have zero consideration for you as a fellow human being."

"Isn't it up to me to decide if you've hurt my feelings?" Samuel laughed gently and played with the soft hairs that were perpetually escaping Melanie's updos.

Melanie processed that for a minute. "I suppose. I'm still sorry, though."

"Apology accepted. Shall we go?" He asked quietly.

Melanie squared her shoulders. "Yes," she said forcefully, still tingling from her head to her toes from that sultry kiss. Surely someone had seen them. She never thought she'd been one to enjoy PDA, but that public display of his affection made her feel empowered. *Look at this handsome man kissing me*, she wanted to shout. *And he's mine!*

As they walked, she began with confidence, though her head was down, eyes focused on the sidewalk. She said nothing, though he could feel her thinking about the kiss, same as he was. He frowned, trying to understand what she must be going through. Her shoulders were tense but squared, like she was trying to muscle her way through a crowd. And maybe that was how she felt. Boxed in, claustrophobic even in the large open space.

He slowly slid his hand into hers. She jumped, and her eyes snapped up to his. The fear in them hit him deep within his chest. He was about to apologize and let go when she squeezed his hand with sudden ferocity.

"I'm so glad you're here with me," she said, eyes shining and determined. "I used to walk all the time. Before...*before.* I loved the park, the trails, the big old trees. I mean, I liked the bookstore and the library more, but I used to like fresh air, too."

He squeezed her hand back. "It seems like you still do."

She smiled and risked a look around. The day was warm, and she started sweating. The weird, sticky pits feeling that only happened in the hot sun. She almost laughed. Sweating! She couldn't remember the last time she'd felt like this. It would've been the year before last—probably.

"I do," Melanie finally replied. "Thank you."

Every time Samuel thought about telling her about James's call, he stopped himself. This walk wasn't about him. Melanie needed this, and if he said something, it might make her more anxious. He was nervous enough. If he ruined the moment by telling her what he'd found, what he suspected, what would that do to them? It would rip them apart. He could handle this on his own. He'd figure it out. And anyway, what would he do if she broke down on the walk? Run to get his car? Did people breathe into paper bags anymore, or was that something they only did on TV?

There was never a good moment. She was either beaming with accomplishment or working hard to get better. And he sure as hell wasn't going to ruin it by opening his mouth.

"We're here," he said and paused on the sidewalk.

She bumped into him, then laughed and twined her arm in his. The action, so small, made his heart swell. Yes, the book stuff could wait. This was Melanie's time.

Chapter 30

"Oh!" The sound fell from her mouth as she looked up. She'd been counting her footsteps to hold repetitive thoughts at bay and bumped into Samuel. The sight before her immediately filled her with awe as she leaned into him. She'd made it, and the prize for her courage lay before her.

A delicate wrought iron fence with a gate that swirled with lace and filigree guarded a house that was mauve and pale pink—which only worked because of its Victorian charm. It was like a dollhouse had come to life.

But it wasn't the house that stopped her breath. It was the riot of flowers—the hills of flowers—pushed against both sides of the gate. Zinnias and roses and sunflowers—and what she thought were peonies and perhaps a hundred other varieties she couldn't name. It was so late in the season, too late, it seemed, for some of these varieties, and that made it more magical, more incredible.

A stone path cut through lush green grass. Melanie noted an

old-fashioned push mower leaning against the porch, and she daydreamed first about Samuel, and then herself, using that quiet instrument of bygone days.

"It's beautiful," she breathed.

"My grandmother loves flowers," Samuel replied. She could feel his eyes on her, could feel them asking what she thought of the house, whether it was too much or too strange.

She could feel the warmth of him near her, too. It felt good, comforting. She leaned back against him, suddenly teary-eyed. She sniffled.

"What's wrong?"

She had missed things like this by not going out. Standing there with Samuel, looking at these beautiful flowers, the stress of walking there sank into distant memory. Maybe she could practice leaving and walking here. It was such a dreamy sight with bees buzzing lazily among the biggest flowers. She imagined how it would look in the spring before it was splashed with color, the beauty of it in the winter with snow covering the evergreens.

Her stomach jumped—she couldn't tell Samuel yet. Not all of it, at least. Maybe when she got to know him better. Part of her whispered that she shouldn't continue keeping things from him, but she shut it out. She was enjoying herself.

"It's just so beautiful. I don't think I've ever seen so many flowers stuffed into one place."

Samuel put his arm around her shoulders and leaned in to press a kiss to her hair. She smelled like books and the outside now, and it made him smile. "Nana will love to hear that."

Melanie smiled, but the twinge of nerves started up again as she walked beside Samuel up the path to the house.

At the threshold, the smell of a home stopped her in her

tracks. It was at once foreign and familiar, and for a moment, panic clawed up her throat.

What are you doing leaving the bookstore, what are you doing here, these are strangers, you don't know them, they don't know you, you'll do something embarrassing and they'll want you to leave. There are germs in there, germs that you've never contracted before, what if you get sick, what if you get everyone at the store sick, what if you get so sick you have to go to the hospital, what if you die, what if, what if. Why did you leave home, why did you, why did you?

And then Samuel had his hand on the small of her back, rubbing gentle circles. "Shhh, *mon petit choux.* They won't bite."

Her body relaxed, at ease under his touch, and a laugh escaped her, "I didn't know you knew French."

"*Un petit peu.* Only a bit," he laughed and leaned down to kiss her and bite at her lips.

She melted into him. She couldn't help it. The scent of whatever he'd put in his hair lingered and sent tantalizing memories of their night together singing through her.

Just as the kiss threatened to turn into something else, they both came up for air, and Melanie took a deep breath. Her head was clear again. The man was a drug, and a potent one at that. She put a hand over her purse. And she had her "extenuating circumstance" meds, just in case.

When they stepped inside, Samuel wondered what he was doing. Nana would be sweet and welcoming, but his grandfather? For the first time in his life, he felt nervous about bringing a girl home. Scratch that. This was the first woman he'd ever brought home. Things were much more serious than he was letting on to himself. He mentally chided himself.

Chapter 30

How could be he thinking these things when Melanie was clearly relaxing and having a good time? Sure, Melanie had her personal troubles, but she seemed to be making such great progress.

An elderly woman greeted them as they walked down a short hallway. Melanie immediately liked her. In her pale blue sweater, grey slacks, and comfy white tennis shoes, she looked like she could be anyone's grandmother. And her warm smile made her feel immediately at ease.

"Samuel, is this the girl?" the woman teased. Facing each other, Melanie could see where Samuel had gotten the shape of his nose and his coy smile.

"Yes," was Samuel's sheepish reply. His ears grew pink. How cute.

"Melanie Montgomery," Melanie said with a great smile before holding her hand out in greeting.

"Oh, my dear, we hug here," Nana said, and embraced Melanie before she could protest. The woman smelled old, like Avon soap, and her papery skin was cold under Melanie's warm skin. It'd been ages since she'd seen her own grandmother, and this felt almost as good as visiting MeeMaw's house.

Chapter 31

Patrick behaved himself at dinner, but Samuel didn't know who wouldn't, as charming as Melanie was. For this being such a big outing into the outside, she dominated the conversation, answering the questions Nana asked, and sweetly handling Patrick's interrogation. He wondered if it was more the out-of-doors that petrified her, as it seemed she was fine once inside a building. Samuel didn't know if that was an appropriate question to ask, though, so he decided to keep the thought to himself unless she offered to explain things further.

The change happened almost imperceptibly during dessert. First, her back got straighter, then her shoulders tensed. When he felt her leg twitch under the table, he took a closer look at her.

Samuel frowned, his brows knitting together. Five minutes before, she'd been giving a dialogue about Victorian literature, but now she looked scared out of her mind. Why hadn't she said anything?

He set his hand gently on her knee and she whipped her head to look at him, turning a wide-eyed glance on him. Her doe eyes would have been sexy had he not felt her fear vibrating off her. "Are you okay?" he mouthed. Nana and Patrick were too engrossed in their conversation to notice.

He saw her trying to figure out what to say or how to say it.

"This is a lot. I'm...." she took a hasty sip of her water.

"Overwhelmed?" he finished for her.

"Yes," she whispered.

He dabbed at his mouth with Nana's cloth napkins. Samuel hadn't missed that she'd wanted to make as good of an impression as Samuel himself had. "Nana, I think it's time we get going. Melanie has work to do tonight."

"Oh! I don't..." Melanie began, feeling badly for cutting their visit short despite her inner turmoil. Nana's perfume stung her eyes, and she struggled to focus on the conversation. She wished she could relax—just be *normal*—but she couldn't and that brought frustrated tears to her eyes.

Samuel squeezed her knee. "Thank you for dinner, Nana. Patrick."

"Yes, thank you," Melanie echoed.

They said their goodbyes at the table, but Samuel paused before they walked out the door. "Can you wait here just a second?"

"I can. And thank *you*," Melanie said softly. She felt like she could breathe here.

Samuel ran a hand through his hair and laughed, though he was beginning to feel anxious himself. "I mean, I'm not a therapist, but it doesn't seem like you should force yourself to the point of pain with these things."

Melanie shifted nervously. She didn't know either. "I'll have to ask Kayla. My therapist."

"I have something for you." Damn, he was nervous. It was just a plant.

"Oh?"

"Wait here."

As Samuel ran to grab Melanie's gift, he had a moment of hesitation. It was just a plant, not a ring, but he was worried after she'd said she didn't want a relationship. Had she changed her mind? Should he feel this way yet? But he knew this wasn't an infatuation, something fleeting that would be gone with the summer heat. He didn't want her to be gone with the summer, with the end of the stacks of books in his grandparents' attic.

When he came back with his offering, Melanie stared at the hanging basket in his hands.

"I thought it would look nice in the store. You don't have anything like that there. And you can take the holder off if you don't want to hang it," Samuel explained, and opened his mouth to continue, then snapped it shut. He was doing the nervous talking thing again. Melanie stood there, face unreadable.

"You got me a plant?"

Samuel felt a strangely sharp pang of disappointment. "If you don't like it or don't have time to take care of something like this, I understand."

Her face lit up. "No! It's not that at all. I'm just...I love it."

Relief he didn't know he needed rushed over him.

She reached for the plant, stroking its long, slender leaves. It rather looked like a spider with a million legs sticking out of it. "You're right, Poor Oliver's needs something like this." Her eyes sparkled as she continued, "And I hadn't figured out plant delivery yet. I'm sure it exists, but this is so much better.

Thank you so much."

He leaned in to kiss her and lingered over her lips. It was just enough to send his head spinning. He pulled back with a grin. "I'll get the car started and cooling off so I can take you home."

Her stomach dropped. She was not getting into a car. "Can we walk?" She squeaked out.

"This is heavy," Samuel laughed. Surely she was joking.

"I have a...thing...with cars," Melanie said lamely. Oh, God, it was all going to tumble out.

"It's just...cars are outside. I haven't been in one for so long. I don't want to go there yet," she quickly said into the silence.

"How do you get places? Did," he corrected as he stuffed his keys back into his pocket.

The innocent question stabbed at Melanie inside.

"I ride my bike," Melanie lied. "Rode," she corrected.

Samuel felt the fear coming off her like heat waves off a dark building in summer. "Okay, we'll walk," he said with a smile.

They left the house and walked in silence for a few minutes when Melanie blurted out, "It's agoraphobia."

Instead of jumping into conversation, Samuel remained quiet, feeling the comfortable weight of the hanging plant at his side and waiting for her to continue at her pace.

"Do you know what that is?" She asked with a sideways glance at him.

"I've heard the word before. Can you tell me what it means to you?"

And it poured out of her. She'd told him about the fire, but now she told him about how the changes had seemed logical at first, how she'd taken time away from the outside world to help as they rebuilt, how it consumed all her time, how it just

157

became easier to stay inside. She simply quit thinking about going outside.It became a threat again when someone would mention going somewhere. Or, she would forget the cats were gone and try to feed them only to realize they'd perished and it was her fault.

And then, and then, and then.

"And then I just never left," she finished as they neared Poor Oliver's.

"But now you are," Samuel replied.

Melanie felt her gut twist up. "How will I ever get to where I was? Look at how hard this was, and I still had to leave early!"

"But you did it. Isn't that what's important?"

"I guess."

"Melanie."

She looked at him and he pulled her to him in a hard kiss and tried to say everything to her with his lips that he didn't know how to say with his words. He knew in his heart that Melanie would be alright. She was so strong, so capable, so smart. If only she could see that.

When he pulled away, he saw something raw and pure shining in her eyes, and when he whispered goodnight in her ear, he could have sworn that she let out a breathy laugh, something that sounded happier than he'd ever known her to be.

Chapter 32

The day after walking to and from Samuel's grandparents' house, she couldn't get out of bed. Her legs and hips ached, and her head hurt from the sun. She walked around the store all day long; she shouldn't be this sore.

But as she lay there in bed, she understood the truth of it. It took walking—*walking* of all things—for it to hit home, and that hurt so damn bad.

She couldn't get out of bed. She just couldn't do it. And with it being Sunday, she could lay there and justify it.

Stay in bed, skip her meds, skip the pain reliever, skip the water for her parched throat, and skip the aloe for her sunburn. How long had that walk been? Twenty minutes there? Thirty back?

Melanie felt the hot, flushed skin of her nose, cheeks, and ears, and the fair skin of her decollete. As much as she probably needed the sunlight to help her vitamin D levels, this wasn't the way to accomplish it.

What would happen if she got out of bed? Usually, she would take the time to outline the possibilities of her day before she went downstairs. The routine of it soothed her.

Her heart dropped. What if it wasn't simply routine? What if she was stuck? Even as she thought it, she knew it was true.

The desire to check on Samuel's gift finally pushed her out of bed—the plant really did look amazing in the front windows. She also needed to gather information about Hans' book purchase. And what Samuel said last night...how he'd looked at her...

Yes, she could do this. She *had* to do this. She wanted desperately to see where this would go with him.

She stared at the plant soaking up the sun. This was now its home. Here it would get watered, and drink in sunlight and air. It wouldn't move from this spot unless it started to decline.

Maybe it was like her. Had she been declining by staying inside?

The fatigue, the lack of desire to leave, the anxiety: perhaps they *were* indicators that her time inside was finally taking its toll.

"I think I need to get this figured out once and for all," she said to the plant. It didn't respond, of course, but she knew Samuel would.

She'd mentally practiced walking outside fifty-two times and had her head poked out the back door when she saw Samuel strolling down the sidewalk. She watched him walk—just casually walking down the street like a normal person. Her legs still hurt, but getting up and about had helped.

She melted into his embrace when he reached the back door. "I was trying to meet you down the street."

Samuel soothed his hands over her shoulders and pressed a gentle kiss into her hair. She smelled like the sunshine she was trying to step into. "I'm willing to bet that sunburn hurts. Would it be better to stay in until it heals?"

She leaped at the chance to stay inside. "Probably. I just....I think I need to keep going out, desensitize myself."

Samuel pressed more gentle kisses to the top of her head, then followed her inside. "If that's what you want, love. What is it you needed?"

You, her heart cried. But instead, she said, "Someone to talk to. About what I'm going through. I think I'm going to go see my therapist."

She picked at the skin around her thumb. She'd have to talk to Kayla about that, too. When she realized what she was doing, she slid her hands in her pockets, though the urge to pick at them remained.

Samuel held his hands out for hers, and she reluctantly pulled them from her pockets and set them in his. He gently ran his thumb over hers. "You don't sound happy about it. It looks like your poor thumbs need it, though," he squeezed her hands, but she drew them away.

"They do. I do," she said.

"Do you actually want to go see your therapist, or are you just thinking about seeing them?" Samuel asked, and Melanie had to look away from the intensity of his gaze. It made her want everything all at once. Him and his body, his company, going out, traveling, driving. Going places. Leaving. All of it.

Melanie took a deep breath and let it out, feeling the energy humming between them. She couldn't lie to him anymore. "I want to go. I've just...gotten stuck."

"Time told me that there's a fine line between a routine and a rut," Samuel said quietly.

Melanie opened her mouth to make a smart retort, then snapped it shut again. She had no sassy comment for what she knew was the truth. She could have sworn he read her mind. How could he know that she'd been thinking that very thing earlier?

"I'm in a rut." Melanie breathed it out so quietly, she wasn't certain Samuel heard her.

But he had. "I wore myself into a rut in real estate. Did it so well, I didn't even know I was in up to my neck before I started drowning."

She went hot and cold as she listened to him, feeling what he was saying so keenly that she thought for a moment *she* was the one doing the talking. He took her hands again, holding her there with the strength that simply radiated from him.

"I just kept...*doing*...day in and day out. I was good at the work, so I kept at it. I buried myself in it until I couldn't see anything else. And you don't have to worry about other girls," he said with a laugh, "because I couldn't hang onto a girlfriend to save my life, even if I'd wanted to. I was too busy working in my own world."

That bit was different, she thought, and a small part of her was happy he didn't have strings and old attachments out there.

"And it didn't matter where I was," he continued. "Paris, Vancouver, Brisbane. I worked myself into the same numb place every time."

"How did you stop?" Melanie asked.

Samuel thought about that. What had changed? He'd been taking on clients and closing deals and having a good ol' time with David in between. But he hadn't been looking any deeper than any of that. "I chose myself," he finally said. "I quit

162

choosing things that weren't helping me be...*me*."

"I just want to be normal," Melanie said.

Samuel took her hands and shook them gently. "Don't. Don't say that. You're not broken, or whatever it is you're trying to say. You're taking life at your pace. If it's different from mine or the Average Joe, who cares? They're not you."

Melanie absorbed everything he said, feeling something blooming within her. She *could* do this. Maybe it would take some time, but she could choose herself just like Samuel had.

"I should probably go work on paperwork," Melanie said into the comfortable silence between them.

"And I have some errands to run." Samuel reached up and traced the soft curve of Melanie's jawline, and played with the wisps of hair that had already escaped her topknot. A few curled ringlets lay gently on her shoulder. Even learning something so small about her stole his breath.

"Could I go with you?" Melanie ventured, fighting the inevitable surge of panic.

"It's something I have to go do by myself." Which was true, so why did he feel like a jerk for saying that?

"Oh. Okay," Melanie said with a smile, but it looked forced, and Samuel had the feeling he'd made a misstep, that he'd cost her something. He didn't know what else to say, so he kissed her and left.

Chapter 33

As he drove out of town to Second Day Books, Samuel couldn't shake the feeling that he'd bungled something. He hadn't lied that he needed to take care of this himself, but Melanie was involved in this, too, thanks to him.

Had James Young given him the appraisal anyway, despite his better judgment? It had arrived at his grandfather's house in the mail the day after James called about the books' potentially sordid pasts. Samuel had passed it along to Melanie without mentioning the call.

He didn't like confrontation. In fact, he couldn't think of anything he liked less. If that made him a coward, well, so be it. Pushing a sale was one thing. There was a thrill in maneuvering a person or couple through the ins and outs of purchasing their first home or first vacation home on the shores of the Mediterranean. There was a thrill in talking them through the purchase when there were multiple buyers, negotiating with the seller and finding their pain points. But if someone asked him to confront an angry seller or angry buyers? He'd rather have taken a sharp stick in the eye.

But he needed to do this. If not for himself, then for Melanie.

So, when he drove out to Second Day Books and marched up to the front door, he was surprised when he yanked on the door and it didn't budge. He tried pushing, feeling like *that* kind of ass, but it didn't give either way.

Then he saw the "Closed for Renovations" sign taped neatly over the store hours. He stared at it dumbly for a full minute before it clicked that there were and would be no renovations currently happening at Second Day Books.

There'd been zero communication since the appraisal had arrived for *The Great Gatsby*. The email itself hadn't contained anything except the attached appraisal. He'd had no follow-up phone call and had heard nothing more about the suspicious history of the book. Samuel hadn't submitted any of the paperwork James Young had suggested he needed to verify the book's life.

Genius that he was, he hadn't questioned it. He'd forwarded it straight onto Melanie.

Icy fear ran down his back.

He called the number listed on the appraisal and could vaguely hear it ringing inside the building. He looked up Second Day Books on his phone and called the other number listed, and that one rang inside, too. He'd had James Young's email, but he had a sneaking suspicion he wouldn't get a response there either.

And Samuel had thought himself the coward.

Samuel called his friend and lawyer, David, and left him a message that there was an urgent situation that required his attention. He could still make this right, but he needed to act before that sinking feeling told him he was already too late.

Restless and without answers, he drove back to Warren full of growing worry. He would get this figured out, but in the meantime, he wanted to do something for Melanie to help soften the news. He'd need help, and he knew just the people to ask.

Chapter 34

She counted her steps all the way to the counselor's office. Eight blocks. Four-thousand, eight-hundred, and ninety-eight steps. Her legs ached, but they weren't cramped, at least. Melanie let out the breath she'd been holding for the last quarter block and read the sign on the door: *Kayla Koerner, LCSW*

The tree in front of the building had grown since Melanie had been there last. A lot. Guilt gnawed at her insides. The tree had her full attention now. It'd been at least a year since she'd seen it. Had she disappointed Kayla by not coming regularly?

Going inside the building eased some of her fear, but it was so different from Poor Oliver's. The smell wasn't sterile like a hospital, but it was clean. It was an office with no books. She'd gone to the Walnut Café and Samuel's grandparents' already. This was a third place.

Progress.

It was progress.

The knot that had wound itself up inside her gut slowly

unraveled throughout her session. She hadn't seen Kayla in a year and was grateful to be back. Why had she stopped?

She was on the verge of asking when Kayla asked, "Do you feel a difference between teletherapy and in-person meetings?"

"I like in-person much better," Melanie admitted.

"What about it do you like better?"

Melanie took in the office's soothing neutrals that made her think of the ocean. She fidgeted with the weighted stuffed bear sitting on her lap. It soothed her as much as the room. "I do like people, you know. And new places. I just hate leaving. It feels better if I just don't think about it, as if the outside just doesn't exist."

"You haven't been here in quite a while."

Tears sprang into Melanie's eyes. "I haven't left home much."

Kayla sat quietly for a beat, prompting Melanie to add, "I haven't left at all."

"How did that make you feel?"

"I feel safe at home."

"And when you leave or think about leaving?"

"It's awful. I've been trying to leave, but everything outside is so overwhelming. The smells, the sounds, all of it. If I leave, something might happen again. Or I think the cats will get out, then I remember the cats are dead, and I did that. I did that to them." Melanie felt her heart rate rise, felt the full force of her thundering pulse. Then, the palpitations started. "I th… I think I'm having a h-h-heart attack," she stuttered.

Kayla looked at her calmly. "What do you feel?"

Her adrenaline skyrocketed. Her palms were sweating. She looked at the door. Why wasn't Kayla freaking out? Or calling 911?

Melanie gasped for breath. "My heart. I think I'm having a

heart attack."

Kayla reached out and held Melanie's hand. "You're not."

"I am."

"You're having a panic attack."

"I feel like I'm going to throw up."

"There's a trash can right next to you." Kayla gestured at it. "But I don't think you need it. Tell me what you *feel*. What's your body doing right now?"

"I'm having a heart attack."

"No, what do you *feel*?"

The room twisted in a slow, sickening spin. "My heart is beating fast. I'm sweating. I can't breathe. My mind is racing. I'm so dizzy. I'm going to pass out."

"You're having a panic attack. Look, we've been talking for two minutes now and you are still here, right?"

Somewhere in her panicked haze, she realized that she *was* still there. "I'm still here," she said quietly.

"What do you feel now?"

Melanie took a deep breath. She was alive. She wasn't dying. "My heart isn't beating as fast. I'm not that dizzy anymore. My palms are still sweating."

"Your body is experiencing those things, but you're still here."

Melanie nodded, felt the dizziness leave her. They continued to talk, to work through her feelings until they all but disappeared. It was a magical moment when they disappeared. She felt like she could take on the world.

"Will they be gone now?" Melanie asked hopefully.

"Part of what we do here is to keep exposing you to things that bring on the panic. Since leaving home at all is one trigger, part of your homework is to go outside as much as possible until I see you again next week."

"I don't like thinking about that."

Kayla nodded. "I know. But do you *want* to do it?"

The answer was easy. "Yes." A year ago, her answer would've been, "No." Melanie felt different now.

"That's good."

Melanie breathed deeply, pleased to find that her chest wasn't being squeezed anymore. "I thought about going over to Samuel's after this. It's only a few blocks. Even just to walk by and look at the flowers. His Nana has a beautiful garden."

"That sounds like a great idea," Kayla said with a smile.

Chapter 35

Samuel's plan was coming together better than he could have hoped. After seeing her fight with the old cash register a dozen times, he started asking as many probing questions as he could without letting her in on what he was thinking. He glanced over at the front counter where a new touchscreen checkout sat. From what he could tell from the questions he'd asked, she was open to transitioning to digital. He could tell her his suspicions about *The Great Gatsby* and James Young's store at the same time. She could hold the appraisal if she needed to. Not that he was tempering bad news with good news—it was just how the situation had worked out.

He tried to ignore the bad feeling he had about waiting so long to talk to her.

He checked his watch. Anna Jane had come over to keep Melanie company upstairs while he worked some magic. And Anna Jane was happy to accept a bribe in the form of agreeing to help her out when she needed an extra pair of hands across the street. That she seemed to think Samuel was going to be around long-term made him feel hopeful for his future with Melanie.

He owed Anna Jane big time. And he was pleased with the result. Chloe's idea of the flowers and plants was genius.

White roses, he'd decided, were much more romantic than red, and they looked better against the books in Melanie's favorite section of the store: the Victorian classics. Electric candles were nestled into arrangements with the roses and greenery. The candles in the clever lanterns that Chloe had also found threw a pleasing glow against the spines of the books they sat before. It smelled like a heady combination of books and nature, a musky, earthy scent Samuel wouldn't have ever caught himself thinking was sexy.

Until now. Until Melanie.

Who would have thought that a few short months ago, he would meet a woman who made him feel like he was a teenager again, who drew out the Samuel he'd been before stuffing himself into suits and slacks purposefully a half-size too small?

He grabbed a short stack of books from the pricing table and headed up the stairs. Melanie had to think he'd arrived only a few minutes before. He was pleased with her open look of excitement when he stepped into the kitchen. She and Anna Jane were at the table.

"I found a few that look interesting. You'll let me know when you've priced them? I want them. Hey, Anna Jane."

Taking his cue, Anna Jane stood and stretched. "Thanks for the chat, Mel. I think I'll go with the wood-backed chairs again. Much more homey."

"You're welcome," Melanie said. "But I thought you were convinced you needed those funky metal ones?"

"Guess I'm feeling fickle. Bye, guys!" Anna Jane skipped down the stairs and out the door.

Melanie shook her head. "She's being weird."

Samuel shrugged and held out his book stack. "You'll let me know if I can have these?"

"Do you even read?" Melanie teased, but pored over his choices with obvious interest. A Civil War history, a biography on Ayrton Senna, and several obscure sci-fi titles that she thought might end up as fifty-cent paperbacks.

She saw his face redden adorably. "I really like reading; I just didn't have time for it before. They crammed *How to Win Friends and Influence People* down your throat, and while it was a great book, it wasn't...very imaginative."

"What's your favorite book?" Melanie's eyes sparkled with interest.

"Don't laugh at me," he said, alarm apparent on his face.

"Never," she replied quietly. "Books are much too serious for that."

"*Lord of the Rings*. The series, I mean."

The response warmed Melanie's heart. "Well, that's nothing to be ashamed of. That's a lot of peoples' favorite."

"I know it's just a popular novel, not like some obscure rare book."

Melanie was touched by his shyness. For each layer of him she learned about, she liked him more. "It's not my area of expertise, but there are lots of rare copies of *Lord of the Rings* out there. First or custom-bound editions, out of print copies, signed books. There could be something rare or unusual or unique about any book."

Samuel laughed. "That makes me feel better. Thank you, Melanie."

She got on her tiptoes and gave him a chaste kiss on his temple. "Anytime you need to pick my brain about books, I'm happy to talk."

"In that case, I have something about books to show you. Well, sort of about books."

"Oh?"

He grabbed her hand. "Come downstairs with me." When he saw the question in her eyes, he continued, "Inside. Here. We're not leaving."

"Okay."

He saw surprise in her eyes when she hit the last step and saw what he'd done to the back part of the store in between the table displays and bookshelves.

"What's all this for?" she breathed. There were white flowers everywhere, interspersed with electric candles and lanterns. Delicate greenery wended its way over and around the tables and displays and bookshelves. There were so many dozens of flowers, she couldn't count them all. Somehow, he'd transformed the spot into a Victorian garden. At least, that's what it looked like to her.

It was breathtaking and wonderful and...oh, God, was he going to propose? Once the thought was there, it wouldn't leave. Proposals led to weddings, and a wedding meant marriage, and then he'd want her to move into his place, and she'd have to leave and what then? She took a deep breath and held it until her vision greyed. She would have to say no and break his heart. As much as she'd been trying, she couldn't leave here for good. Just the idea of spending the night somewhere other than her place broke out a cold sweat.

"It's for you," he said quietly, his palms becoming clammy. Suppose she wasn't understanding about the books? Suppose she would think he'd been involved in his grandfather's mistake? "I wanted to thank you for everything. For helping me relax, for being the reason I've found, well, purpose here in Warren." Could she hear in his voice how much he meant it?

His words touched her deeply, in that place she'd tried to squash down the week before. "No one's ever done something like this for me before." She took it all in with wide eyes. "It's beautiful."

"You're beautiful," he murmured, and pulled her into his arms.

Then she saw what he'd set up at the register. "What's that?"

Samuel released Melanie from his arms and pushed her gently toward the counter. "Go see."

Where she expected to see the register was a sleek white machine with a swivel touch screen. Heart pounding, she slid a finger across the screen. It lit up to a home screen with her name and Poor Oliver's and what looked like limitless check out options. She could track everything almost effortlessly with this kind of a system. She could get low stock notifications before she had to scramble when a customer asked for something, and it was gone. This would save her so much time.

"Samuel," she said, unable to get anything else out.

When she turned to him with her eyes so shimmering and bright, he almost couldn't speak.

"What's all this for?"

"It's for you."

"But...why?"

"Because I love you."

The silence that hung in the golden air burgeoned with the enormity of their confession. It seemed that magic shimmered in the rose scented air, magic that she wanted to hang onto as long as she could. Forever, if she could find a way to bottle it, to keep it tucked near her heart.

"I love you, too."

He reached for her as she pushed him against the bookshelf and pressed herself against him, feeling the roughness of his jeans against her bare thighs. A skirt had been an appropriate choice that day, though she wasn't sure either of them had anticipated this explosion of primal desire. Right now, she didn't want gentle. Right now, she wanted to feel.

Samuel's hands reached up her shirt, and the calluses on his hands drew shivers from her, her skin prickling with goosebumps. When his cool fingers found her breasts, she gasped, unable to form a single thought. She became desire, desperate with want, as he gently rolled her sensitive nipples between his fingers.

"Samuel," she gasped, gripping him tightly. She'd never experienced such intense desire.

He pushed her shirt up and pulled it over her head while Melanie wrestled with the small buttons on his shirt. Watching his chest expand for breath was captivating. Once she conquered the last button, she pushed his shirt off and trailed kisses down his sternum and across his chest. He was perfect, his skin hot beneath her cool lips.

Melanie let her hands wander down Samuel's torso so she could tuck her fingers under the waistband of his jeans. They locked eyes, and the rawness that Melanie saw reflected back sent butterflies fluttering inside her.

"Samuel…"

He pressed her hand over the hardness inside his jeans and Melanie quivered with want. "I want you, Melanie."

"Now," she finished. Heat rushed through her skin and deep inside her body. She answered by kissing him again and again and unfastening his jeans. The *need* for him made every touch agonizing—she had to have him now.

Samuel pushed her skirt down and she kicked it the rest of the way off.

They both paused for breath, and she watched Samuel's eyes flicker over her body. She didn't feel the usual burn of self-consciousness.

Samuel's breath left him in one great whoosh. Even for the night they'd already spent together, he was wholly unprepared for the vision that stood before him. He trailed his hands over her shoulders, her arms, her sides, lingering over each curve. Melanie Montgomery was simply the most beautiful woman he had ever seen.

"Did you know that your hair gets ringlets in the humidity? Just here," he said as he touched the shorter hairs at the nape of her neck. And then, because he couldn't help himself, he leaned in to graze his teeth over the spot where her neck met her shoulder.

Melanie closed her eyes and moaned, feeling the touch to her very core. "I mean, I did, but I didn't know anyone else had noticed them. They're so frizzy. They won't go away."

"Don't make them," he murmured as he sifted his fingers through her hair, letting it spill over his palms so that it cascaded across her shoulders. "They're adorable."

Her skin was more golden in the soft glow, and when he spied a trail of freckles near the top of her left breast, he couldn't help but lean in to kiss them, to worship the skin they dotted.

What could she say to that? "Thank you" just didn't seem

right. She arched her body into his kisses, awash with pleasure. Closer and closer until maybe he would feel what she wanted so badly to say again. What if he had proposed? Would it be so bad to say yes?

She wanted to find out.

Somehow, they made it upstairs, laughing and stumbling in their rush to keep their hands touching smooth muscle here and delicious curves there. Melanie tugged him toward her bedroom, but Samuel pulled her toward her cozy movie nook. Together, they tumbled into the nest of blankets between the bookshelves.

Melanie knelt over him, kissing Samuel's temples, his cheeks, and then, finally, his lips. She noticed for the first time the grey in his hair threading between his dark waves. Charmed, she ran her fingers through his hair and fingered the grey streaks.

She took in the sight of him there leaning casually on his elbows, the sparse hair on his toned chest, the dark trail of hair that led to his manhood. He was perfection and he was *hers*.

"Do you have…?" she started, then choked on a giggle as she realized that she didn't have a condom. She *could* waltz out and get some, but that would kill the mood. And imagining ordering them on Amazon for rush delivery threatened to send her into full on belly laughter.

"What's so funny?" Samuel asked huskily. He'd find a way to throw himself out the skylight if she was laughing at him.

"I don't have condoms here." A giggle escaped her. "But I can think about going out to get them without melting down. But then…but then…" She lost herself to giggles.

Samuel pulled her into a hard embrace, "My sweet, silly girl." God, she was beautiful, and flushed with laughter and desire, he wanted her even more.

He reached for his pants and extracted the object in question. Melanie took it and tore it open. Before she placed it on him, she grasped him in her hand and bent down to take his erection into her mouth, tasting him. Samuel's sharp intake of breath almost sent her over the edge—the things he could do to her without even touching her—and she moved to slide the condom over his hardness.

His hands grasped the flare of her hips as she straddled him and slid down onto him. They mutually gasped at the pleasure and pressure as she rocked her hips against his. She squeezed his hands over her hips, then ran her hands over her body, felt her own curves, the swell of her breasts, her heaving chest. She heard him call her name, breathed in the books and him, and fell into the canyon of time.

Chapter 36

When he woke in the morning, he had five missed calls from David and three from James Young at the bookstore. James Young who had conveniently been unreachable before this. Trying not to disturb Melanie, he slipped on his briefs and walked downstairs to wander through the shelves. At four in the morning, the late-night crowd was home, and it was silent outside. The electric candles glowed dimly in their lantern houses, and Samuel was struck with a wave of guilt. He'd justified not telling Melanie everything for so long now that he wondered if he could handle it without her ever knowing. Merely thinking that crested fresh waves of guilt. It *had* turned into the circus he hadn't wanted.

He called David, knowing that he was calling him too late. At the first whiff of this business in the other bookstore, he should've called David right then and there. He should've sat down with Melanie, too—everything else be damned. Now it was a mess, one that he wasn't sure he could unravel.

Chapter 36

Reliable David answered after one ring, even though it was just after five his time. Samuel skipped straight to the issue. "There's some trouble here."

"Real estate, women, or both?"

Samuel laughed and raked a hand through his hair. He caught a look at his reflection in the front window. Against the hazy darkness, he could see his hair stuck up chaotically, and…when was the last time he'd shaved? He'd have a proper beard in two more days at this rate. "Property. Stolen. And a woman, but she's not involved. I mean, she is, but not like that. Argh!"

"And you're involved how?"

"It's a Patrick Reid Special. Books this time."

"So, what you're doing isn't legal."

"I'm not doing anything."

David scoffed. "Well, you did it whether you realized what you were doing or not."

David knew the thin line Patrick Reid had skated in the past. Stories of the man in his prime still circulated up north, even making their way to Vancouver. The comical mismanagement of funds during the '70s that somehow had escaped the highest levels of scrutiny. There was probably a good reason why he'd decided to settle quietly into a no-name town in Kansas for the remainder of his retirement.

"And you got roped in? Doesn't sound like the Sammy Reid I know."

Samuel let out a noise of utter frustration. "I should've told him I'm retired and left it at that."

"So, tell me about it. I can get out of here in a couple days."

Samuel told him what he knew. He had a sneaking suspicion there would be more by the time this was all over. And the entire time he could only think about Melanie.

He would figure out what to say, he just needed more time. David would know what to do.

By the time he slipped back into the nook, the sun was shining, and everything seemed like it would turn out just fine.

It was three agonizing days before David got into town, and by then, Samuel was calmer than he had been. This would get sorted out without becoming a circus, and everything would go back to the way it was before.

The ride from the airport was quieter than he wanted, but he didn't know what to say. David filled the silence with comments on the quaintness of the rural view beyond the city.

"You don't see this much space every day."

Samuel remembered his descent into the area. How much had changed since then. "Flyover states look a bit different from the ground."

David shuddered. "This might appeal to you, but it gives me the creeps. Give me a forest of skyscrapers any day. You can get lost in this big sky."

Samuel hummed at that, kept a good grip on the wheel. He was keyed up from the two hours of sleep he'd managed to scrape together over the last forty-eight hours, and too many cups of coffee he'd drank to compensate. And none of them from Walnut Café because he'd surely run into AJ and spill everything. No, he needed to talk to Melanie first. And soon.

"What do I do?" Samuel asked.

David tore his eyes from the scenery. "You go to the police first, before anyone else does. We need that good faith gesture that you're not involved while we untangle whatever's going on here."

"And tell them about James Young."

"The bookstore owner? Not yours, the other one," he said to Samuel's sharp look. "Yes, we'll address that."

Not much later, David and Detective Huff sat with him through the entire story, taking notes and 'hmming' and nodding appropriately.

"These are quite serious charges you allege, especially if we find out you were involved knowingly."

Fear that he'd never felt before gripped his limbs. He felt like he was in a nightmare, and he couldn't move. "I wouldn't be here if I knew what was going on. I just want to get this sorted before…before…" *Before the woman I love gets hurt,* was what nearly tumbled out of his mouth. "Before my grandfather gets himself in more trouble over this. I can't pry anything out of the man."

Detective Huff grunted and kept writing.

"How will this work?"

"Mediation, I imagine?" David directed his question to the detective.

"Oh, yes, that's the likeliest scenario. We'll do some checking into this James Young, with Mr. Reid—Mr. Patrick Reid, that is—then we'll contact you. We will certainly need your help to piece everything together. Do you have any records of what's been going on?"

"I was working on my quarterly taxes when I found out something wasn't right."

The detective nodded. "Good records will help. I'm going to make some inquiries. We'll be in touch, Mr. Reid."

They shook hands and Samuel left, feeling worse than when

he'd arrived. Guilt, betrayal, fear: they all formed a hard rock in his gut. This wasn't something he could work out at the gym, nor was it something he could smooth over with Melanie over a meal or, worse, with a book.

By the time they reached their brunch spot, Samuel was about to jump out of his skin. He was surprised that David had waited this long to say anything more to him. Was his friend adding that much sugar and cream into his coffee just to draw this out?

"I've got to talk to Melanie."

"She's your bookstore owner?" David questioned, knowing the answer. He traced the chipped edge of the plate that housed his sinfully delicious biscuits and gravy with one finger. What a charming and quaint town this was. They'd been chumming it in the big cities for so long, he'd forgotten that his friend had any roots in a small place like this.

She was more than that, Samuel thought, and he knew David would see beyond his guarded reply. "I'm...involved with her."

David was surprised at his friend's coolness. Not that they were prone to divulging details of their conquests, but Samuel had never been one to withhold anything before.

"Involved? How clinical," David replied, knowing that prodding outright wasn't likely to get him any details. Samuel was brooding into his coffee and picking at his omelet and waffle. "She must bore you to tears."

Samuel huffed, but didn't take the bait. The truth was, he was terrified. He didn't know how he was going to talk to her about this without looking like a complete jackass himself. He'd been had by his own grandfather. His grandfather!

"You know," David continued. "As your lawyer, it benefits you to be candid with me. On all matters."

184

Chapter 36

Samuel sighed and took another sip of his coffee. "You aren't going to stop, are you?"

David speared another bite of biscuit. God help him, he was about to order another serving. This place was a gem. "You know me better than that."

Chapter 37

When Melanie saw Officer Bird come in, she thought he was there on a break for some coffee. She was at the counter, arranging the last of the white roses from her night with Samuel. She felt light, happy. And though she hadn't heard from him in twenty-four hours, she felt confident that she could stroll to his house if she wanted to. She could think about leaving without melting into a panicked puddle. Not that it felt *good*, yet, but she was willing to give it more time.

But Officer Bird stopped to talk to her instead. "I need your help," he said, setting a piece of paper on the counter.

It was a list of books. *Rare books*, she thought, and furrowed her brows. *The Woman in White* was on there, as well as a specific edition of *The Picture of Dorian Grey*, then *The Great Gatsby*. There were others she didn't recognize but would have loved to have—an early Poe with few known copies, some lesser known titles like Margaret Oliphant's *A Country Gentleman and His Family* and Braddon's *Lady Audley's Secret*.

"We're investigating stolen books," he said.

Melanie wasn't certain she'd heard him correctly.

"I'm sorry, what?" The words came out far sassier than she intended, and the affable Officer Bird's eyebrows nearly disappeared into his hairline.

"Well, we're investigating on behalf of someone else. You're not named in the suit," he said hurriedly to Melanie's open-mouthed shock.

Melanie snapped her mouth shut and swallowed the lump in her throat. Her ears started ringing. Whether that was the Viibryd or the all-hands-on-deck warning now coursing through her, she couldn't say. "I...do you need this for research, or do I need to call a lawyer?"

"These things always require paperwork, but the people involved prefer mediation over a lawsuit."

Lawsuit? Mediation? The words might as well have been Greek to Melanie. The ringing in her ears was definitely adrenaline. It was hard to concentrate on Officer Bird as it grew louder. And had the room just shifted?

Melanie felt the beginnings of a fainting spell coming on. Contrary to all Victorian literature, it was not a graceful matter and usually ended with a black eye or a nasty bruise somewhere on her person. She gripped the counter and slowly took a breath. Maybe she could stave this off. "So, you need to know if I've seen these books?"

"Yes, and if you've sold them since. Your records, you know. The process you use to buy and sell them."

Melanie felt the air leaving the room, and she sank down in the nearest chair. If she stayed upright, she *would* faint. "I usually check every book that comes in. I mean, you know, against the popular stolen lists. And these were all appraised. I don't know how one could have gotten through, let alone two. I do everything by the book. I just don't understand how...I don't understand."

"Well, we'll need...Miss?"

A realization dawned on her, prickling her scalp and slapping her like a cold splash of water. "Oh my God, I know these books."

She stopped herself before she said, *I know who brought them in.*

Heat replaced the cold, and she felt it rise in her face and bring tears to her eyes. Her mind went everywhere at once. Were the appraisals forged? Had he really spoken to James Young? Or perhaps this was all James Young's doing. Did Samuel know?

Did Samuel know?

Officer Bird watched her with kind but openly curious eyes. "Were they brought in recently?"

The heat was already starting to form into something that felt harder, something that she had never felt before. It ripped through her usual cyclic worries, replacing them with a white fury she'd never known. "The two I know came in within the last six months."

"I'll need to know everything you know. You understand?" he asked. "Start with a list of the books and the books themselves."

Melanie closed her eyes, remembering the report she'd filed during the fire, the shock she'd felt when she'd started down the basement stairs and discovered it was flooded. She'd stood on the steps, water up to her calves, dumbfounded until Officer Bird had found her.

"The water has to go somewhere," he had said simply, but

not unkindly.

"The basement was full of antiques," she'd said dumbly. "Books. Rare ones."

"I'm sorry," he'd said. "We'll need a list of all of it. I imagine you'll need it for your insurance, too."

One could not simply replace the irreplaceable. How was she supposed to close up the hole she felt opening, the one where Samuel had fit so neatly? She'd thought she'd done a fine job of it after the fire, but look at what that had gotten her. And now. And now? Everything she'd been working so hard at was unraveling right before her eyes.

Chapter 38

Melanie looked up from a pile of books in too poor of condition to put on Poor Oliver's shelves. She wasn't sure if they should even go to Goodwill. She saw Samuel and some suit walk in the doors and the anger that hit her was swift and deadly.

"Paul, man the counter, please," she said.

She barely registered his 'Yes, ma'am,' as she stomped away, mind racing a thousand miles an hour.

She was so mad she didn't even register that she still gripped a handful of to-donate paperbacks. Her knuckles were white.

"Samuel Reid! How dare you come here after what you did!"

Rendered speechless, he blanched at her words. Melanie stalked up to him and shoved a finger at his chest. He had the audacity to look hurt.

"The police were here. *Again!*"

Samuel's face fell. Good.

The suit smoothly took over before Samuel could open his mouth to talk. "I'm the representative for Samuel Reid."

"Why can't Samuel tell me that?" She glared at Samuel.

"Because I'm his lawyer. David Hanley. Samuel thought he wanted to tell you something, though I advised him against it. So instead, he has something he needs to tell you. Samuel?"

He didn't have the words. Any words. He didn't know what to say. 'Sorry' would sound trite and worthless. And David had made it clear that 'sorry' wasn't to be uttered.

He felt the heat of her stare, and this time it wasn't from passion. Someone else had gotten there before him. And the worst part of it all was that even if he did know what to do, David had told him not to *do* anything. It didn't matter if he wanted to go to her, or wanted to explain—or run away like a coward.

"I came here to tell you that they're going to file a motion to take the books."

Melanie's ears were ringing so loudly she didn't know if she'd heard Samuel or read his lips. "You're too late! The last two days have been a nightmare! You have no idea how many calls I've gotten—I'm being audited!" She ticked the list off her fingers. "I've already gotten an email motion from someone else. Probably the original owner of the books. The ABAA is doing their own private investigation too. So don't you dare come rolling in here like you're trying to save me or something. You're too damn late."

Samuel struggled to find purchase. "When I found out, I tried to get David—my lawyer—to get it all sorted before there was an issue. I didn't want you to be involved."

Melanie felt the color leave her face. "You *knew?*"

Samuel felt the already boggy ground he'd been on give way beneath him. "I mean…I didn't. Until I did. James Young called—"

"*James Young?*" she screeched.

Samuel looked terrified. "Yeah, we'd been communicating ab—"

"Oh, you're *friends* with that jerk?"

"I'm not friends with him, but when I took the book... books...in for him to appraise—"

Her mind raced. "Did you and James Young concoct this plan together? What were you doing, trying to get me shut down? How many more books are there? What was it?"

He was sinking so quickly into the mire that he didn't know how to get himself out. He scrambled for footing, only to feel himself slipping further in. "No, I just...my grandfather—"

"Don't try to blame this on anyone except yourself."

"I didn't know what he was doing!" Samuel shouted.

"That's the biggest load of crap I've ever heard!" Melanie exploded. "How could you *not* know? With all those books, those *insanely* rare titles? They don't just show up at estate sales!"

"I should've told you when I thought something was wrong. But by the time I'd found the extent of it, it'd gotten out of hand." Samuel raked his hands through his hair nervously.

Melanie plowed ahead, fueled by her anger and her new-found ability to leave on her own. "And now I could lose my store, my home!" she yelled.

"I'm..." he got out, eyes blazing with hot tears, desperate to apologize. "It's a mess, and I don't know what to do now! I didn't realize how high the stakes were!"

She didn't have a reply save for the blinding fury churning inside her. "Stay away from Poor Oliver's. Stay away from me. Keep your dirty books away from here. Send them back where they *rightfully* belong."

"Melanie, what else do you want me to say? How was I supposed to know what all I was into?"

"Open your eyes!" She yelled, clutching the books to her chest. "Why else would he have been giving you those books to sell? How could you not see their condition, their obvious excellent quality and deduce that they weren't really from his attic? How could he have boxes and boxes and boxes of rare books without you noticing once that they were even in the house?"

Samuel glanced at the top of the stairs and then stared at her. "As hard as a child realizing that his grandfather is a thief. You tell me why I can't be in denial about that, and then we'll talk about you living in the attic of a bookstore."

A flash of heat rushed across her face. "Get out."

Samuel began stuttering to get something out, but Melanie shook her head, her mouth set in a tight line, lest she say something she really regretted. She clearly didn't know this man as well as she thought she did. "Get the hell out. How dare you come into my home and spend time with me, and then spit on my life."

"Melanie, I—"

"No! Get out! I don't want to hear it!"

"I can fix this," Samuel pressed. "I can pay you back for the revenue you would've had from the book—the books."

The fire in Melanie's eyes had warned him before, which was why the coldness that suddenly replaced it hit him so hard. "You think I care about the money? Is that what you think? That I'm in this for the *money*?" She threw the books at him. He didn't have time to react before they hit him square in the chest. He jumped back, stunned.

"I shouldn't have let you come here." David took Samuel's

arm before anything else happened. "I think it's time we leave. Miss Montgomery?"

"What?" Melanie hissed.

He hoped there weren't any other books in her reach that she could launch at him. "I'll be in touch via email."

"Please do," she replied vehemently, then turned around and stalked inside.

When they left, Samuel felt shaken and nauseated, like he'd eaten a bad sandwich from the deli in Vancouver. He knew this wasn't a puke-and-feel-better situation, though. This was worse than he ever could have imagined.

"Why couldn't you just email her the motion?"

David couldn't have hidden his shocked expression had he cared to try. What he'd seen inside the bookstore between the very attractive owner and his friend was intriguing. If he wasn't mistaken, there was more than simple chemistry between the two of them, and he oddly hoped that this worked out in Samuel's favor so they could smooth things over. He had seen worse situations take better turns for couples before. "I never knew Samuel Reid was such a coward."

Samuel took the blow. He knew he deserved it.

Chapter 39

The rain made a unique sound on the front windows of Poor Oliver's. It was one of the many reasons Melanie had put an overstuffed chair there. It was a highly sought after spot by customers to sit with a cup of coffee and a newly purchased book. The chair should have been hideous—its browns and yellows and burnt oranges better suited to a harem in the 1970s—but it worked among the myriad neutrals of the bookshelves. Someday she might move the thing as it really was in the way, but she'd put it there for selfish reasons, too.

Once she closed for the day, Melanie wasted no time locking the doors, dimming the lights, and comforting herself a latte with vanilla syrup instead of indulging in her usual evening decaf Americano.

She bypassed grabbing a book, and kicked off her shoes. She settled into the chair. She imagined for a long moment that the slinky black cat she hadn't named yet would jump up and curl into her lap, but, no. No, he had died in the fire. Why couldn't she get that through her head?

"I'm sorry," she whispered into the quiet. Maybe someday she could forgive herself for not being here for that sleek black cat or his sister. She hoped he'd forgiven her, wherever he was in kitty heaven.

Melanie heaved a huge sigh and stared out the window. The rain pattered against the thick glass and somewhere nearby she heard it gurgling down the gutter out the spout. Here she could finally think, could finally peel back the layers of the days before.

The pain hadn't come yet. She suspected it would, but for now it was simply simmering inside her, somewhere deep down where she couldn't touch it yet. It was a numbness that wasn't numb, and the meds didn't help. To some extent, she felt like she was underwater or in a fog half the time. She felt the knee-jerk reaction to stop her meds again, to retreat into the shop and never emerge again.

But that wouldn't serve her. She would need to leave again eventually, to go places she'd only begun to rediscover.

But she couldn't think about Samuel. Not yet.

Melanie did think about the walk to Kayla's earlier. Actively thinking about going outside had gotten easier, as had the act of actually doing it—even if she didn't want to.

The sidewalks to her therapist were safe. If she stayed on the sidewalk, she was fine. No deviating into the grass that looked so cool and inviting.

She'd gazed out over the park and its large trees. Her heart rate climbed as she thought about what it would mean to step into the grass, though. Mosquito bites, wasps, perhaps even a used needle that she would step on. It would go through her shoe. She would get AIDS and die.

Chapter 39

Melanie had stopped then and pressed her hands against her thighs. She'd felt the fabric, trying to center herself away from such anxious thoughts. Denim, the slight roughness of it, that patch on her thigh that was thinner than the rest because she leaned on that side the most at the checkout counter.

Her therapist had tried to get her to talk about him.

"Avoiding the situation isn't going to make it go away."

Melanie had dug in. "I can pretend like it didn't happen, move on. I'm fine."

"You might think that's the best way to go about it, but the body remembers. Trauma is imprinted on our bodies in all manner of ways, and if you don't face it, eventually it will show itself."

Watch me do it, Melanie had thought then. But now, in the comfort of her home, snuggled into the store's favored chair, looking out rainwashed windows, she didn't believe she could.

Chapter 40

No one else in town acted like they knew what was going on. One day, a pair of officers had come in to collect the books. They took the box and then they were gone. She wanted to feel stupid for mourning the loss, especially of the edition of *The Woman in White* that she'd wanted so desperately to be hers. There was no Marian Halcombe in her that day, no feeling of bravery or strength to stand up to the man who had done this to her. That day she was simply sad.

At least she didn't have to make any appearances in person. She'd gathered everything she could think of they might need, made photocopies, and sent it off through the lawyer she'd retained. She'd had several Zoom calls and emails with her lawyer, but she hadn't had to leave.

AJ drove her to the courthouse to drop off additional paperwork when her lawyer couldn't make it by Poor Oliver's. The car ride had been terrifying, but she'd done it.

The call about the audit had and hadn't surprised her. Sure, throw that in there. More phone calls and more photocopies. At least digging for records was easy thanks to the new system she'd been setting up because of Samuel. She'd considered hauling out the old register and its notecard credit tracking out of spite, but she knew that was childish. He'd given her a great gift, even if he hadn't stuck around to see it.

Three patrons called to be taken off her auto-call list for rare books. Others called with their sympathies but sounded skeptical about ever buying from her again. Her worries were coming true.

The Sentinel newspaper could've painted her in the light as what she was—another victim—but of course they didn't. The reporter had fun with the headline—*Local Bookstore Duped by Senior*—though she didn't find it so funny.

Shannon Jackson called her personally later in the day when she was exhausted from the fallout. She was considering closing early even though droves of people had come through to see the celebrity at the heart of the town's gossip.

"Poor Oliver's, can you hold?" Melanie asked, not sure she could take another call from a reporter pretending to be a patron.

"I'd prefer not to," the male voice replied.

Melanie recognized the speaker, but she couldn't place it. A quick peek at the caller-ID told her all she needed to know. She stole a glance at Jenny, pointed at the front counter and mouthed. "Please?" Then, she said into the phone, "Shannon. How are you?"

"Two phone calls in the same amount of months, Miss Montgomery. People might think we're seeing each other."

Her stomach clenched and she skirted a cluster of customers to retreat into a quiet corner. She wound up between sci-fi and horror where memories of Samuel's burning kisses begged her to forgive him. But how could that ever happen?

"You're only calling me because the ABAA wants you to."

"That's not entirely true. And we all make mistakes."

"Not of this magnitude." Her voice shook. Damnit, Melanie, hold it together. "If I'd just done my research, waited the time I'm supposed to wait before the sale, I'd—"

"Hush. Have I ever told you about what happened to the Jackson who started my store?"

"What, in 1848? No, you haven't."

"This was a bit later in his career, but yes. He unsuspectingly sold dozens of counterfeit copies of the Brontë sisters' novels, the originals, you know, by Currer Bell."

"That was the 1800s. I sold a stolen book that I could've found out about if—"

"I'm not finished," Shannon interrupted again, and Melanie fell quiet. As far as people she respected, Shannon Jackson was near the top of the list.

"Jackson could've folded and caved to the bad press selling those copies brought him. Word of mouth, as you know, was gold in those days."

Melanie ran her fingers down the tattering covers of well-loved Stephen King books. *And it still was in small towns*, she wanted to say.

"It isn't much different, I imagine, from how you've built your own name up in that little town in Kansas."

Melanie felt a smile tug at her mouth while Shannon's words tugged at her heart. "You read my mind."

Shannon chuckled, a charming sound that she was certain someone else would find unapologetically attractive. It made her miss Samuel's husky laugh. God, she wanted to hate him.

He had absolutely no respect for her or himself.

"Jackson didn't let up, though," Shannon continued. "He just kept going. He believed in his books, believed fervently in what he was doing."

"And here you are today," Melanie murmured.

"Exactly."

Melanie sighed. As far as pep talks went, it was spot on. So why did she still feel so sad?

"You need to come see us in New York," Shannon crooned. "Come meet everyone this year."

She held her breath. Thinking about all that entailed sent a spear straight into her gut, though not as sharply as she was used to. Imagining traveling to the airport and boarding a plane blew every circuit in her brain, but the possibility of driving someday? It didn't hit her as hard as those thoughts used to.

"There's a great group of women now. You'll love them. And I'm here. I want to show you around, give you a tour of Jackson's."

Melanie let out the breath she'd been holding. She wanted that, but not because of him. "Thank you, Shannon. I'll come sometime; I'm just not sure when. I've got to get my feet back under me first."

When she finally ended the call, she wandered a bit and stood in numb silence in a quiet alcove with a selection of non-fiction books. She didn't want Shannon. And she didn't want Samuel—not the person he had turned out to be, anyway. What she had left was herself, and that was supposed to be enough. She clenched her hand around the phone. It *would* be enough. She owed that to herself.

Chapter 41

J ust before the mediation began, Samuel tried to keep still as the attorneys were shooting the breeze. How could they be so nonchalant? He felt like his entire world was continuously imploding.

He watched Patrick across the way with the old family lawyer, Vance Pearson. Patrick hadn't said a word to Samuel for days now, though whether that was on the advice of his lawyer or out of pure spite, he couldn't say.

"Hanley."" Melanie's attorney nodded at David over his cup of coffee. Guilt stabbed straight into Samuel's stomach. At least Melanie wasn't there.

They bumped elbows, coffee in one hand, paperwork in the other. "Byergo. Surprised to meet you here. You get around."

Frank Eischens, Delbrook's attorney, nodded at Gene Coberly, the Fitzgeralds' lawyer, "Is your client related to *the* Fitzgerald?"

Coberly shook his head, clearly not feeling like being part of the pre-game festivities. Samuel didn't blame him.

When the mediator, Mark Galus, opened the doors to admit them, Samuel saw their faces change. They became all business as they shuffled in. The knot in his stomach grew.

He'd sat around conference tables like this before, but he was used to being at their head, leading the conversation. Even with David sitting next to him, he felt small and insignificant. And he didn't like it.

Sitting there staring at Jack Byergo across the table, Samuel worried about Melanie. She would've had to go somewhere, been forced to leave the store. Would she have had to box up the books and bring them in? He imagined her putting all those pieces of history into a cardboard box and handing it over to someone who likely didn't know how to handle them. It made him want to vomit.

His grandfather sat with his best poker face on, hands clasped on the table. To the old man's credit, his hands didn't shake, and he had the gall not to look nervous.

As they began, Samuel felt increasingly uneasy as the lawyers chatted back and forth. One of them threw out possible prison time, only to be shut down by his partner since it hadn't yet progressed into a criminal matter.

When they got to Samuel, he thought his heart might crawl out of his mouth and land on the table.

"Why did you engage in the sale of rare books, Mr. Reid?" Galus tilted his head to indicate he spoke to Samuel and not his grandfather, then clarified. "Mr. Samuel Reid. We'll get to Mr. Patrick Reid in a moment."

Samuel cleared his throat and wished for water. He didn't think that would do anything for the panic he was feeling now. Even with David beside him, he felt like he was about to get pulverized. "I was only trying to help my grandfather."

"You were trying to help him sell stolen books?"

Samuel gritted his teeth. "I was trying to help him sell *books*. I didn't know they were stolen. I knew nothing of the rare book trade before I came back to Warren. It's been an eye-opening experience, to say the least."

Galus didn't look amused, and David crushed his heel into Samuel's toes. *Quit being a sass-hole.* "Answer the question," David whispered to Samuel. "Don't offer anything else."

"I had retired," Samuel said. "My grandfather was cleaning out the attic and asked me to sell some books. I didn't think anything of it."

"Do you frequently take your grandfather's word on matters of financial significance?"

"Um, objection?" David said. "This is supposed to be mediation, not an interrogation into my client's motivations for helping his grandfather. Wouldn't we all be in the same boat if our grandfathers asked us for help cleaning out an attic?" He got a half chuckle from Byergo and Eischens.

David took the helm before the mediator spoke again. He folded his hands on the table and said, "I have a proposal that should make everyone happy. We are prepared to pay restitution and reparations. Gentlemen, we can be done with this, short and sweet."

Mark Galus said, "It would be in the interest of all parties to resolve this outside of court." He addressed the trio of attorneys. "Do you need a break to consult your clients?"

Coberly cleared his throat. "No. My client wants to recover his stolen property." He eyed David. "He hasn't decided what comes next, a civil suit or charges—so no deal."

Frank Eischens said, "My client wishes to buy the book outright, but, as that is apparently unlikely, we are amenable to

Mr. Hanley's proposal, which should…" He indicated Coberly. "Make your client happy."

Byergo said, "And my client is willing to negotiate—restitution for time and monies lost."

Samuel couldn't help sitting up straighter. Melanie was willing to negotiate. That sparked a ray of hope. If she was willing to negotiate this, maybe she'd be willing to negotiate with him, as well.

The mediator sighed, and Samuel felt the whole of it in his very soul. "Since there is no obvious or unanimous consensus, we'll break for fifteen minutes."

Chapter 42

When they resumed, Patrick's poker face was gone. He shifted uncomfortably in his seat and looked tired. He blew out a shaky breath and announced, "My boy had nothing to do with this."

The room, already hushed, deepened its silence with the intensity focused on his grandfather. Samuel opened his mouth, but David clamped a hand down on his thigh. He closed it.

Patrick heaved a huge, dramatic sigh. "It was a long time ago, gentlemen—1976—and my memory isn't what it used to be. I recall being part of a group of men hired to help the Fitzgeralds move. As far as I remember, a few boxes were accidentally left in my Ford at the end of the day. I had every intention of delivering them."

He cleared his throat. "But, I didn't—clearly. I was much younger then, you see, and rather lazy, truth be told. Time passed, as it does, and I forgot. We moved to Kansas and everything became boxes. Just...boxes. And many went to the attic. By today, you can bet I didn't think much about them."

Samuel didn't trust a word of it, but still, he held his breath. He could hope it was true.

"It'd been a long time, and no one had called...I figured... well, what was mine was mine at this point and there was no sense in keeping them any longer. We'd sold other things, so it seemed...well, it was time to sell. My boy just happened to be here and he's a mite more able than I am. It was logical to ask him to take the books to sell. I told him how simple it'd be and he agreed like a good grandson. He didn't know. That's all there is to it."

The trio across from him sat up straighter, the collective intake of breath the loudest sound in the ensuing silence. Before they could say anything, Mark Galus said, "Why didn't you say this before the break, Mr. Patrick Reid?"

Patrick crossed his arms. "I had a chat with Vance over the break. He advised me to speak."

David seized the moment to say, "My client's impeccable track record of reporting fraud throughout his career will absolutely remove his culpability."

Relief prickled over Samuel, a feeling that left him hot and cold and almost giddy. He was absolved. His grandfather had finally spoken up and done what was right for once.

The other lawyers' faces became unreadable as stone. The Fitzgeralds' lawyer said, "Confession aside, that doesn't change what we're here to do."

"Did you reach an agreement, then?" Galus asked.

With a nod, Delbrook's attorney said, "My client will return the book and accept Mr. Hanley's proposal."

"And in light of that, my client has also accepted," Coberly said, "and expects *appropriate* compensation."

Samuel felt both relief and nervous energy wash over him as appraisals and numbers circled the table. By excusing him, his grandfather was now responsible for what was not going to be an insignificant amount of money. And he could only hope that the Fitzgeralds didn't press charges or slap him with a civil suit for damages.

An hour later, the negotiations were finished. The mediator summed up the agreements and gave a week for the paperwork to be completed, signed, and filed. And that was that. On the surface, anyway. Samuel still had Melanie to contend with, and that frazzled nerve endings he hadn't known existed.

Would he ever regain Melanie's trust?

Chapter 43

"What am I supposed to do?" he moaned to Chloe over a beer at Rusty's later. The relief from the mediation was gone. All that mattered now was Melanie, but he didn't even know where to start.

"You really didn't have anything to do with it?"

"For love of…no! No I didn't."

Chloe tossed her silvery blonde hair over her shoulder. Samuel didn't miss the looks the guys at the bar gave her, though he knew they'd be sorely disappointed. By both Chloe's choice of partner and her scathing directness. "Then I'd say some groveling is in order. I imagine your knees can take it."

Samuel raked his hands over his face and through his hair. "I hate this."

"Sounds like a personal problem," Chloe said over her drink.

Her tone rankled Samuel's already thin temper, but he kept himself in check. "I really need a friend right now, Chloe. Seriously. You were the biggest help with those lanterns and the plant. I need real advice now."

"I'm serious too," she replied quietly, this time without the bite. "Grovel. Get on your knees. Whatever it takes. If she's meant for you, you'll find a way through."

"I didn't realize you were so wise."

She rolled her eyes at him. "I'm going to thank you for that very backhanded compliment, but you should probably work on your delivery."

Samuel groaned and threw his head back. "God."

"It won't kill you, you know."

"I want to do something meaningful for her. I know she needs more than my words this time."

Chloe signaled for her tab. "If she means that much to you, then give her everything. You aren't going to get anywhere pussyfooting around the situation. Give her everything and mean it."

After they said their goodbyes, he walked into the dark park by the bar. The tall trees soothed him and he gave into enjoying how the wind sang through their branches. Who would have thought the big city boy would land in Nowhere, Midwest? The restless feeling was back, but this time he knew why. He had to suck it up and communicate with Melanie. Tell her everything. Be honest, open. The idea of it made him sick to his stomach, but the thought of life without Melanie Montgomery was even worse.

He had messed up. Big time. In hindsight, he could pinpoint the exact moment things had turned, too. It was the night he hadn't said anything. The first night. He knew now that if he'd just come clean, if he'd just been open and honest with her, they would've gotten through it. All those moments he'd kept his distance, telling himself that it was for her benefit, hadn't done anything but shove a wedge between them.

And if he'd just been open, they would have gotten through it together.

That fact wrenched his heart in a thousand different directions at once.

He paced through the park, aimlessly wandering amongst the tall trees. He paused at one of the tennis courts and stared up at the lights. Something swooped in to snag the large insects flying too close, attracted to the brightness.

Since there was no one using the court at nine at night, Samuel lay down on its cooling surface and stared up at the sky. What he thought were birds turned out to be bats, sailing in to feast on the night's bugs. He watched in fascination at their elegant movements, diving and turning in midair.

The momentary distraction proved to be anything but that. He suddenly thought that he wanted nothing more than to share this moment with Melanie.

Chapter 44

She went to her therapist. She went to see AJ at the café. She worked on piecing together a collection of Victorian mysteries—the more Gothic, the better.

She felt stuck being able only to go to those two places, as though her progress had stagnated with Samuel's absence in her life.

Some days, she wallowed in it, and on others she stomped her way down the sidewalk to her therapist's office, arriving breathless and determined.

She took her medication. She signed the papers from the mediation, not caring to read through them at first, then staying up late to pore over them. She felt nothing about Samuel agreeing to the terms, and then she was happy, and then she was upset. It was all mixed up.

She hadn't sold a rare book since the ordeal. She didn't know if she would again.

She could fool others, but she wasn't going to fool Paul or AJ for long.

And she could count on Paul to push every button she had about it, too. He might've been her friend, but he was one of the least sensitive people when it came to her issues.

But it would be so easy to fall into a relationship with him. Paul would live there officially, and eventually become her partner in ownership of Poor Oliver's. There would be a big wedding with family and mutual friends. They would live together upstairs in her—their—bookshop apartment for quite a while before they'd need more space. They might have children, buy a house a few blocks away. She would find a way to relocate there. She would stay home, or he might, and the other would continue to run the business. Their children would go to school and grow up. Paul would go on fixing, mending, painting, building. She would go on selling books—it'd be her corner of the world. It would be perfect. Stupid and perfect.

But Samuel.

With Samuel, she could leave every now and again, turn the reins over for a week to the hourly employees and go see another city, another state, another country. He'd said they could go to New York, to the book fair, hell, to see *New York*. She hadn't even thought she really wanted to, but now that it was out there, all she wanted to do was be part of something bigger than herself. If she loved books so much, why not open up her world to more of them? Why not learn all she could for the more educated clientele, for herself?

Oh, but he had lied to her. And for how long? Maybe from the minute he walked in the door? Some part of her murmured deep down that perhaps he hadn't. That perhaps he hadn't known, but she stifled that part and topped it firmly with a lid.

"Are you moping?"

The voice startled Melanie so much that she let out a shriek and dropped the bookmarks she'd been idly flipping through at the front counter.

She whirled around. "Dammit, Paul!"

He grinned and shrugged. "Situational awareness much?"

"Asshole," she muttered, though without any malice.

Paul set a box of what Melanie assumed were the new store shirts on the counter. "Were you though?"

"Moping?" Melanie knelt to pick up the bookmarks, losing herself again in their cute Victorian lace corners, which reminded her of *The Woman in White*, which reminded her of going to New York, which reminded her of Samuel, which... she stopped herself. "Yeah, I guess I am moping."

"You need to quit wasting your time," Paul argued. "I hate seeing you be sad over someone who did what he did."

Not that she'd told him exactly what Samuel had done, but there was enough stir about it around town that he probably knew the gist. "It wasn't a waste of time. He's just at a different place in his life."

Paul looked angry. "Nice thing to say about someone who did you so dirty."

Melanie shrugged and heaved a huge sigh. "What am I supposed to do except pick up where my life left off? I'm busy here. Over my head, if you must know. I have more than enough to do."

Paul lifted an eyebrow. "That was a really long-winded version of, 'I think I'll get stuck in my rut again.'"

Guilt stabbed at her immediately and she flushed with remembrance of Samuel saying the same thing. Funny, she thought, how different their tactics were for talking about her issues. "Listen, thanks for your concern, but I'm moving on."

"Okay," he said sarcastically. "If you won't quit wasting your time being stuck inside, then at least stop wasting your time on him. I hate watching you be sad."

And that was it, Melanie realized. Paul was sad for himself when she was moping, not her. He was too young, too immature to understand yet. She hoped he would someday. "If I said that my PTSD and anxiety and agoraphobia were a waste of time, then I'd be giving into the darkness. I'm not saying I don't wish I could have lived life without them. I do. But if I say they are a waste of time, that the time I spent with them is lost, then I'm saying those moments in my life don't mean anything. And they mean so much. They have shaped me into who I am today."

Paul scoffed at her, and she felt a hard knot of resentment form inside her.

There was a darkness on Paul's face that she hadn't seen there before. "Why don't you just stop being so dramatic? Just quit being afraid of it."

For all the pushing he'd done, he'd never gone this far, and it hit Melanie with an icy force she wasn't expecting. She opened her mouth to speak, but Paul beat her to it again.

"You're putting on a show, and it's embarrassing. Do you want him to see you like this? Just get over it, move on, leave, go places. That's what'll teach him the best lesson. Get over yourself and him."

Face hot, Melanie turned away from him and yanked the box of shirts off the counter. What swirled within her wasn't guilt for her situation, but anger at Paul's assumptions. There was a time where she might've been reduced to tears by his words, but that was before. Before Samuel. Before therapy. Before she'd believed in herself. "Please go back to Spear's or wherever you were before you waltzed in here. Please, Paul. I am really not in the mood."

"Listen, if you want to hang around here and keep throwing yourself a pity party, be my guest." And with that flippant statement, he left out the back door, and would probably forget in five minutes how much of a dick he'd been.

Paul didn't get it. He was too young, too inexperienced, too immature. Samuel got it. Somehow, without being told, he knew the right ways to push her. He hadn't made her feel like she was being forced outside her comfort zone.

Was her life better with him or better without him? And if it was better with him, how would she begin to open up to him again, or even talk to him?

She drank more coffee that night than she had in quite awhile, and paced the shelves in a quiet desperation as she moved through the mire of her thoughts, filtering out what was true and what wasn't.

No, she didn't love Paul, not like that. She loved Samuel. She had messed up, and so had he—oh, yes, he had—but what did that matter when she felt good all the time with him? They could move on, be happy, maybe fight occasionally about something stupid, but then they would forgive, forget, and be happy again.

Something was bubbling up inside her, something that made her feel rather lightheaded. She had to leave, find Samuel, tell him that everything was going to be fine.

At the front doors, she paused, and closed her eyes when her breathing and heart rate began to speed up. If she left, she was not a terrible person. She would lock the door and no one would get in, and she would come back and everything would be in one piece. Nothing awful would happen. Everything would be fine. The park was only a handful of blocks away, and since it was early Sunday morning, there wasn't much traffic yet.

She was going to do this. For herself. She didn't *need* him or anyone to walk out into the sunshine on her own.

Taking a deep breath, she pulled the door shut, latched it, and didn't look back as she stalked off down the street.

Chapter 45

The mediation had gone more smoothly than Samuel could have hoped. He'd signed the paperwork and washed his hands of it. His agreement to Melanie's terms was all but forgotten for Patrick's assumption of the blame. But even for that, all Patrick Reid had to do was return any money received in a sale, pay restitution, and never sell a book again. It was a comparative slap on the wrist to what Samuel had been expecting. Perhaps it was the small town mediator, perhaps it was the luck of the draw with the lawyers present. The other books were retrieved and disappeared into the hands of some nameless benefactor who couldn't have known their worth. And thanks to Samuel's meticulous record keeping, the return of funds and payments went so smoothly it was almost as though none of it had ever happened.

Except for the resentment he felt toward himself.

Samuel spent his days taking care of Nana and trying to shield her from the worst of the fallout.

And working through his own shame and embarrassment.

He sat on the porch with his whiskey and the sunset while he chatted on the phone with David.

"Come back to Vancouver, man," David was saying. "Start fresh."

Samuel swirled the ice and whiskey, then sipped. "It's not that easy."

David scoffed. "Since when has my jetsetting friend not thought that literally everything was easy? I mean, remember that last trip to Paris? Twelve hours' notice and we were on the plane and ready to sell three hours later. Don't tell me it's not easy."

The man had a point, Samuel thought as he surveyed the lawn in the waning light. But he felt as though he'd become attached to this place. Nana would need help clearing her garden beds and getting the outside ready for winter. The house needed a fresh coat of paint. He'd begun putting down roots without even thinking about it. He tipped the glass back and drained the last of it. "I'll think about it."

"Do. I think you'd be better off here, clear your head away from things."

"Is that your advice as my lawyer or my friend?"

"Both," David replied, his tone serious.

He did give it serious thought, but there always seemed to be something that prevented him from leaving. An interesting art show at the co-op, live music at the artsy bars, and a feeling of closeness with the town that he oddly hadn't felt in Vancouver. Perhaps that was just the way it was in small towns. Days passed between readying his grandparents' home for the fall and falling in love with the town. How could there be this much to do here? Perhaps it was the university influence, but there was enough art and culture and food and historic sights to keep him entertained indefinitely. He tried to relax and enjoy it, but there was always something missing, some tension beneath everything he did.

The last thing he expected was to see her out and about.

He'd gone to the last Concert in the Park, the headlining band a minor '90s sensation that had sounded like a decent way to spend a few hours. There she was in her skinny jeans, chucks, and cropped top, laughing with AJ while they sat on a blanket and listened to the band.

It just about killed him, but he was glad that she had the courage to be out in the world. His heart wanted to leap out of his chest. This was it. This would be the moment he spoke to her. He could feel the pull to her, though she hadn't seen him yet.

And then Paul appeared. He sidled up to Melanie and set his hand in the small of her back. She laughed at something he said.

It was as if his entire world was crashing down. How stupid of him to think that—it already had.

Of course.

They were best friends, had known each other for years. And now that she was out and about, Paul would be there for her. He would keep helping her out and now she could help him, too. There was no place for Samuel in that. Samuel who had only been in her life a few months and had given her nothing but trouble. It was all so clear.

And then Samuel wanted nothing more than to be out of town.

He went home to pack, but promptly dumped everything out of the bags.

No, he wasn't giving up.

Chapter 45

But he was going to give her space.

He picked up the phone. He'd been thinking since his conversation with Chloe, and he knew what he had to do now, no matter what it cost him. And if Melanie still wanted him on any level, he could start by putting a foot in the door. Or a book in the door, if one wanted to look at it that way.

Chapter 46

It was like she'd suddenly discovered that she had a superpower, one that'd been dormant her entire life. She didn't *actually* need anyone's help. She could give herself permission to go somewhere, and she could do it. Just like that.

Samuel might've cracked the door for her, but she had kicked it wide open. So, with a rush of confidence that was coming easier each time, she put the 'Back in 20 minutes' sign on the door, locked up, and headed over to the Walnut to get a latte and snack. No depending on Paul or AJ to bring it over anymore.

"I'm getting used to you stopping by," Anna Jane smiled as Melanie strolled up to the counter.

"It smells so good over here. I don't know why I waited so long." Melanie smiled, but Anna Jane didn't see the smile reach her eyes.

"You miss him," Anna Jane said quietly.

"So much." The lump in her throat wasn't anxiety. No, this

felt so much worse. How was she going to take back all the things she'd said to him? And would he apologize for what he'd said? She'd been agonizing over it for weeks. When to call him or whether to call him or whether he was in town at all.

Anna Jane thankfully didn't push the subject while she made Melanie's latte. The two planted themselves at the table by the window. From there, Melanie could see Poor Oliver's. It was strange to see it from the outside, like she was having an out-of-body experience. As she sipped at her latte, picked at her muffin, eyes on the door to her store, she supposed in some way, she was.

"Jackson's has been calling a lot."

"Like *that,* or just professional?"

Melanie didn't look up at her friend as she scraped at the dried lipstick on the side of her mug. "Both, I think. But I don't want that. He's found out a lot about what happened."

Anna Jane 'hmm'd' over her own coffee.

"Books were stolen from a small collection back in the '70s. Forever ago. The only reason they know about it was from a newspaper story and a folded piece of paper sitting in the library. Like, it had literally been sitting there for decades."

"Where?"

"Some nowhere town in Michigan where Samuel's grandfather used to live. It was a private collection, but after the owner died, most of the books had been marked to go to the library. Seems they went missing somewhere between the home's estate sale and the library."

"What happened to the books?"

That hurt almost as much as what Samuel had done. She felt her voice go rusty, "They go to any living family, who can do whatever they want with them, since it wasn't expressly stated in the will of the private collector."

Anna Jane saw the pain in her friend's eyes. She wondered if Samuel knew how much those books meant to Melanie. Even Anna Jane didn't understand it completely. "Can't you do something about it? Like, an appeal?"

Melanie took a deep, shaky breath. Her nose was running now, and she carelessly wiped it on the sleeve of her chunky sweater. "I can write them a really nice letter and beg for the books. I don't know how they'd give them up now though. As soon as they get them appraised, they'll know what treasure they have."

"If they do that."

Melanie rubbed her tired eyes. Tired of worrying, tired of crying. "I don't know how they won't after so many people have gotten involved. They probably already have. I've gotta get back over there. Thanks for the coffee."

Anna Jane hugged her friend and watched as she headed back across the street. Another figure, also familiar, slipped into the door of Poor Oliver's just behind Melanie. Anna Jane hoped Samuel was there to grovel.

Chapter 47

She returned to Poor Oliver's through the main doors. When she turned around, there was a short stack of books on the front counter that she hadn't set there before she'd left. Every once in a while, patrons would pick up books and abandon them elsewhere, but she didn't think anyone was in the building. She needed to make sure it wasn't a new abandon that she needed to price.

When she got closer, she realized what it was. *The Woman in White* that had been taken from her, taken because of what Samuel had done, tied neatly with a white ribbon that mocked and beckoned her at the same time.

Curiosity getting the better of her, she untied the ribbon with uncertain hands and flipped open the front cover of the top book.

And saw a slip of paper with something written on it.

Thank you for showing me how to look beyond the cover. I'm sorry. -S

Her heart thudded unevenly. Anger tore through her first,

then sorrow so cutting it nearly broke her. Now, faced with the reality of seeing him again, everything rushed up within her at once. And maybe she missed him, but she was *mad*. When she looked up, she saw him moving toward the back door.

As soon as they locked eyes, he turned away and hurried out. He must not have thought she would see him.

"Oh, no, you don't," Melanie said and moved to follow him outside. She wanted to bring the set of books with her, hurl them at him in the street. She imagined it so clearly in her mind, she nearly did it. Instead, she grabbed a handful of paperbacks off the cart as she rushed outside. He was nearly across the street when she caught up to him.

"Samuel Reid! Coward!" She threw the words at him along with all the hurt she felt inside her heart.

When he turned, she threw a book at him. It glanced off his shoulder and fluttered to the ground like a wounded bird.

"Ow!" She saw his eyes track to her hands, looking for ammunition. She threw the other two books, which opened into the wind and fell to the ground like dying birds, their pages ruffled.

"You're lucky I don't have more!"

He rubbed his shoulder, "Are you here to beat me or talk to me?"

The anger she'd been keeping in finally lashed out. It didn't matter if he had been unwittingly involved. She was furious. Chest to chest with him now, she poked a finger into his pec. "I had to go places! The police department! The courthouse!"

"Melanie, I..."

She threw her hands up and cut him off. "I went outside for *you!*" she shouted.

"You should be doing that anyway!" he shouted back, his own anger up now. God, he loved this woman, but damn him if he didn't also see how small her world had become. And she was better than that. She had the talent and charisma to do anything she wanted. She just had to take the first step. If they had to shout about it, so be it.

Her eyes blazed brightly, the amber in them shining over the brown. They were molten now. "Not if I don't want to!"

"Jesus, Melanie! It's not good for you to stay in there!"

"What the hell do you mean by leaving stolen goods on my front counter with love notes scrawled inside?"

"Listen, I didn't write in the book; you would actually hate me for that. And I just…I'd rather leave town for a while than cause you more trouble here. Give you a clean break."

"Leave?" She was stunned momentarily, as though him leaving Warren hadn't been a possibility. But of course, Toronto, or wherever else he had a place, he could go. Then, the anger swelled again, the hurt behind it a raw and bleeding wound. "Run away, you mean! Hide from your problems, pretend like they aren't there, throw money at it until it's gone!"

She'd stung him with that, and he felt it in a place that no one else had been able to touch. "*You* aren't doing yourself any favors by staying in there! What about New York? What about your dreams?"

Tears blazed in her eyes now. "I know!" she screamed. "Tell me about it! I know!" She turned back toward the store and burst into tears, sinking down to the wooden stoop.

Samuel huffed out a huge sigh and sank down to gather her into his arms, where she went without a fight. She felt too slight in his arms, but once there, in his embrace, he felt the rightness of it. Her, tucked near his heart. It was where she was meant to be.

When she finally quieted, he stroked her hair soothingly. "I won't leave if you want me here."

She sniffed, "I want you here. But I'm still mad at you. You should probably go before I throw another book at you."

"You can throw as many books as you want at me if you'll stay in my arms like this."

They were quiet for several minutes, just sitting in each other's arms. Melanie's sniffles quieted.

"Can we bring your little table out here and eat something?" Samuel ventured.

He felt her tense up, then relax. "That would probably be good for me."

"But do *you* want to do it?"

"I need to do it," she replied quietly. Then, softly, "I'm terrified."

He waited a moment. He knew he wasn't supposed to reassure her. "Trust yourself," he simply said.

She tipped her chin up to look at him, tears shimmering on her eyelashes. But he saw the determination there. She could do this. He knew that, and she knew that he had confidence in her.

"Okay," she said softly, a shy smile playing at her lips.

He lost his heart to her again and wondered just how many times in his lifetime he would continue to lose it to her, to lay it willingly at her feet each time she showed her gentle strength.

He leaned in to kiss her forehead tenderly.

"It's getting cold outside," she said.

She was cute when her nose was all crinkled up. "It does that," he replied.

It brought a smile to her face and she took his hand and

pulled him inside. They settled on the couch upstairs and pored over takeout menus without deciding on anything to eat.

"I'm sorry I yelled at you. And threw books at you. In public." She blanched. She wouldn't have been able to do that a few short months ago.

"I deserved it," Samuel murmured into her hair.

"Tell me one thing."

"Anything."

"Where did you get those books? How did you get them back? Or are they another set? I just—"

"I phoned the new owner and offered them an absurd amount of money. I couldn't see them going to anyone except you, Melanie, not after seeing how much you wanted them, how happy they made you. *The Woman in White* belongs to you. And I'm sorry I didn't say something right away. I'm so sorry."

She wouldn't cry again. "How could you? I mean…?"

"I handled it. With David. And there's something else."

She looked up at him with shining eyes. What else could there be? What else could make this moment more healing?

"David called me earlier today. James Young's out of business."

She didn't know what to say. "I don't understand."

"Seems he knew there was more going on than he let on to me. He shouldn't have ever even given me the appraisal. He was trying to set you up to fail. David's been doing some digging and we filed against him shortly after the mediation. He won't ever appraise or sell a rare book again."

Melanie expected to feel angry or triumphant or something big at the revelation, but it simply felt right. Some great weight had been lifted from her in that moment. She threw her arms around Samuel and buried her face in his neck. He smelled so good, like hard work and his cologne, a bit like books, and a lot like home.

He returned her hug, cradling her warmth against him. He was never letting her go again.

Exhausted but comforted, she fell asleep curled up against him on the couch. He didn't have the heart to wake her to order food—this was all the sustenance he needed for tonight.

Chapter 48

When he woke, she wasn't next to him. A quick check of her apartment and it was clear she wasn't anywhere on the second floor. As early as it was, he didn't think she'd be downstairs yet, but he checked anyway.

She wasn't there either.

"Melanie?" he called out softly to the empty building. Only the dehumidifiers replied with their low hum and drip.

Worried, he tried both the front and back doors of the shop. Locked. He went back upstairs and stood in Melanie's kitchen, mulling. A soft noise above him gave him the answer.

It took Samuel a minute of searching to find the roof entrance. Past the space where Melanie watched her movies was a short set of metal stairs. He climbed up and was greeted with a cracked door. Relief flooded him when he stepped through the door onto the roof.

She stood there wrapped in a blanket, the morning sun rising for her, the glory of the Flint Hills behind her. This morning, they were wrapped in mist, and he felt instinctively that autumn was coming. Melanie turned to him and he was hit again by her beauty. The mussed hair, the sleepy smile. He wanted them forever.

When he approached her, she turned and leaned back against him, letting him hold her against his chest. The moment was full of the sounds of the town waking slowly, even for the serenity of the hills beyond. A dog barked somewhere, and the sound of early morning traffic was a soothing rush.

The sun rose above the tall trees, spilling its golden light over their dark green lushness. It was the kind of deep green which would soon give way to reds and golds and yellows. Autumn was near, ready to take the heat and humidity with it. He felt himself missing this moment already, as though it were long past.

"Why haven't we done this before? This view is spectacular." Samuel felt a rush of pride in the place he'd gone to school, something he'd not felt when he'd been here before.

"It really is," Melanie murmured.

"What does it look like in the winter?"

Melanie felt where this was going. "It's cold," she finally said. "But still beautiful. When it snows, you can watch it rolling in from the west, like sheets of snow. I've seen the rain do that, too."

"I want to be here for it. I want to see the fall and the winter and the spring with you." And as he said it, something fell into place for him. These were the words he had been missing before. This, and not changing Poor Oliver's—unless she wanted to—or forcing her to leave if it wasn't on her own. This was what she needed.

"Samuel," she said, feeling off-balance. Something twisted in her stomach. "I may change, and I might not. If you don't like me for how and who I am right now, then—"

"I love you," he interrupted.

"I don't think you heard me," she said.

"I heard you," he replied. "And I love you. I love you here in the bookstore or out there in the world. I love you everywhere."

"You sound like a Dr. Seuss book." She laughed through shimmering eyes, hoping so hard it hurt.

He laughed and turned her to face him. Her eyes searched his. "And what do your favorite Victorian novels say about moments like these?"

Melanie was surprised she didn't feel nervous or anxious about the question, not like she had on the night with the roses. She'd had to go through all she'd gone through just to arrive at this moment. Change, growth, a new life. She could embrace it now.

"The gentlemen profess their love," she said. Yes, this was right. This was the moment she'd been waiting for, had struggled for.

Samuel took her hands in his. The hands he wanted to hold as long as he drew breath. His heart told him how right it felt. "I want forever with you, with these books. This place you've built for yourself, I want to share it with you, make it grow."

"Legally."

"Yes, always."

And she pulled him into a crushing hug, relishing that this man, this wonderful man, was all hers. And now that she had chosen herself, she could give herself freely and accept what he gave in return.

"I want all that. I want to travel with you," she whispered as he hugged her, as though it were a secret. "I want to go places."

"By car or plane or train or horse?" he asked into her hair, breathing deeply the scent of her, the intoxicating mix of woman and books and coffee.

She laughed huskily into his ear and caught the lobe with her teeth, making him moan. "All of them. All of them and more, with you."

"Let's go to your book conference. Whatever year. When you're ready."

She pulled back to look up at him, trust and love shining from her brilliant eyes. "I love you, Samuel."

Samuel bent down to kiss her trembling lips, then pulled her into another hug. "You are my rare find, Melanie Montgomery. I love you, and I'm not letting you go."

She laughed for all the joy in her heart and shifted to tug at his hand. "Come on, let's go across the street for breakfast. I'm starving."

Forthcoming from M.K. Deppner

F ind out what happens after *A Rare Find* in the second book of the Small Town Hope series...

Anna Jane—AJ to anyone who knows her well—has her restaurant, her routine, and only her small-town worries to keep her busy. And that's how she likes it. She doesn't need flashy. She doesn't need sparkle.

David Graves is a bossy, nosy, swanky east coast lawyer who doesn't fit in in Warren. And AJ knows as soon as his shiny shoes get dusty, he'll be jumping on a plane and heading back east. They literally have nothing in common. At least as far as she's concerned.

So why can't she get him off her mind?

* * *

Her days were a pleasant routine. She loved the hard work of keeping the café running smoothly and efficiently, and anyone who might suggest that she needed some time off was met with the wrath of a passionate woman who loved what she did.

She could deal with hiccups and issues better when she handled things herself. It was less that she was controlling and more that she was terrified to lose the charm and personality she'd worked so hard to imbue in the place. Her place. And with her best friend right across the street, she was living the actual American dream.

"Anna Jane?"

She'd been so lost in thought and final closing tasks that she hadn't seen David Graves come in, impeccably dressed despite the hour. She checked her watch and frowned. Five minutes until closing. Even an out-of-towner should know better.

"It's AJ," she said. Samuel's swanky lawyer friend had come into the Walnut Café no less than six times since he'd been there defending his friend's honor, and she was finally feeling comfortable enough with him to let him know her preferred name.

David seemed to take it in stride. "AJ. What should I try today that I haven't yet?"

AJ set a stack of saucer plates down carefully next to the bakery case. "You know, there are other restaurants in Warren. Good ones."

"Are you telling me I don't have good taste…in your own establishment?"

He had her there, but she recovered quickly. "You're here such a short time. Would be a shame not to see what all Warren has to offer. It's not all mom-and-pop restaurants. Variety is the spice of life, as they say." And when had she turned into her grandmother, spouting weird, old-fashioned proverbs?

"I think there's plenty of spice here. And class and excellent food, for that matter." His dark eyes followed her as she bent to move a giant bag of coffee beans out of her way.

She didn't take the flirtatious bait. She did not have time for a fling with someone who would be gone in a week. Plus, he wasn't what usually attracted her. And she didn't think he'd be much into wrestling around in bed with her. He seemed more the missionary type.

She was tall, but he stood eye-to-eye with her when she straightened back up. And didn't back down from her glare. "I get that we're quaint and fun, but I'm sure you're anxious to get back home."

"That's pretty harsh criticism. I don't know whether it reflects more poorly on me or you." David poked through the cellophane-wrapped goodies she'd put out on the tiered end-of-day tray with his soft hands and neatly manicured fingernails.

Lawyers. She almost laughed out loud. But she hated that he was right. And when had she decided to turn this into an argument? She wouldn't say she had a temper, but she could say that she took crap from no one.

"I'm not from your world," AJ said firmly. "And this flirting thing isn't going to work on me."

"You act like I'm visiting from another planet."

"You might as well be." She scrubbed at an invisible smudge on the glass of the baked goods display.

And then he smiled. It wasn't a fake smile either; it was one hell of a genuine smile that lit up his already handsome face. And he was handsome. Any woman who fancied the male species could see that. Styled hair, clean-shaven, wore a suit like nobody's business. Well, he must know that he could make women's knees go weak with that trick. AJ wasn't going to take that bait either, though.

"I bet that works even in the courtroom," she said saucily.

David laughed, and AJ was dismayed to find that even his laugh was attractive. "You're the toughest customer I've ever had, in any case."

AJ slapped her cleaning rag down on the counter. "You must be used to women just falling all over you, no questions asked."

His smile stayed, but she saw his eyes go sly, devious. "I'm sure I wouldn't be the worst decision you've ever made."

She didn't know whether to be mortified or impressed. "Well, thanks for the offer, but I'm not that easy. And we're closed. Thanks for stopping by."

David grabbed a wrapped muffin off the tiered tray to the right of the register and tossed a five down on the counter. "Think about it. See you tomorrow," he said with that sexy smile before he let himself out the door.

AJ put her hands on her hips and stared after his retreating figure. See her tomorrow, would he? Well, if that were the case, she knew just the recipe she'd have to whip up for him.

About the Author

M.K Deppner lives under the rustling cottonwood trees in the Midwest, near the Flint Hills where *Photographs of October* and *A Rare Find* are set. You can find her enjoying a hot mug of tea while writing amidst the chaos of a home with three cats, two step-daughters, and her partner.

You can connect with me on:

- http://www.mkdeppner.com
- http://www.instagram.com/mkdeppner

Subscribe to my newsletter:

- https://mailchi.mp/7ccc7d04f30f/yonpb7efe2

Made in United States
Orlando, FL
18 April 2022

16932678R00134